RE-ELECT NUTTY!

★★★

★★★

★★★

RE-ELECT NUTTY!

★★★

by DEAN HUGHES

Atheneum Books for Young Readers

Atheneum Books for Young Readers
An imprint of Simon & Schuster Children's Publishing Division
1230 Avenue of the Americas
New York, NY 10020

Copyright © 1995 by Dean Hughes

Designed by Michael Nelson
The text of this book is set in Times New Roman
Manufactured in the United States of America

10 9 8 7 6 5 4 3 2 1

Library of Congress Cataloging-in-Publication Data
Hughes, Dean, 1943–
Re-elect Nutty!/by Dean Hughes.—1st ed.
p. cm.
Summary: Nutty runs for a second term as student council president against his arch-rival Mindy and encounters dirty tricks.
ISBN: 0-689-31862-6
[1. Politics, Practical—Fiction. 2.Schools—Fiction.]
I. Title.
PZ7.H7312Re   1995
[Fic]—dc20   94-1776
CIP
AC

★

For Norman and Betty Stafford
—D.H.

★

chapter *1*

Nutty Nutsell was walking down the hallway at school when Orlando Ortega came running toward him. Orlando slid to a stop and gasped, "Hurry, Nutty. You're not going to believe this. Come on!"

Orlando motioned for Nutty to follow, and then he spun and ran back up the hallway. School was over for the day and the halls were emptying, but Orlando dodged and weaved through the remaining kids.

Nutty loped along behind, but he couldn't imagine what Orlando had gone so nuts about.

Orlando grabbed the boys' room door, jerked it open, and then looked back for Nutty. "Hurry," he whispered, mostly just mouthing the word.

Nutty was leery now. What could be such a big deal in the boys' bathroom?

But Orlando hurried inside and opened the door to a stall. Then he whispered, "Okay, step up on the toilet and get your ear as close to that grate up there as you can. Then *listen.*"

Nutty did as he was told, but he couldn't hear anything. "Listen to what?" he asked.

"Be quiet. Just keep listening."

Nutty followed directions again, and he soon heard laughter. Girls' laughter.

"Can you hear them?" Orlando asked, his voice still full of excitement.

"Yeah. So what? It's just the girls in their bathroom."

"Listen to what they say."

So Nutty listened. But he only caught a few words. Someone said, "That's a laugh. He . . ." But Nutty couldn't hear the rest. He waited, but he only heard someone laugh again, and then he heard a door bang.

"They're leaving," Orlando said. "You missed it."

"Missed what?"

"They talk about stuff in there. Private stuff. I heard them say all kinds of things."

"Like what?"

"It was Mindy and Sarah and a bunch of those girls. And one said, 'I don't know why you even wear one. You don't need to.'"

"So what?" Nutty climbed down from the toilet.

"Don't you know what they were talking about?"

"A coat, I guess. No one needs a coat this time of year."

"Nutty, you're so stupid. What do girls *need* to wear or *not* need to wear at our age?"

Nutty pushed his way out the boys' room door and Orlando followed. "Ribbons in their hair, I guess."

"No, Nutty. They—"

"Orlando, I'm kidding. Okay? I know what they were talking about. But what's the big deal? We all know what they're wearing now. We don't have to hear them say it, for crying out loud."

"But I didn't know they *talked* about stuff like that."

"Why not? We do."

"Lay off, Nutty. You're just jealous because you didn't hear it."

"Yeah, right, Orlando. The rest of my life I'll feel bad because you got to hear the girls in the bathroom and I missed out."

Nutty hung an arm on Orlando's shoulder, and the two walked down the hall. Nutty had always been taller than Orlando, but he had now hit his big growth spurt and seemed to be shooting up about an inch a minute. He was a good six inches taller than Orlando. The boys were both twelve and had just started their sixth-grade year at the laboratory school on a college campus in Warrensburg, Missouri. They were a rather strange-looking pair—Nutty tall and blond and freckled, and Orlando short but strong, and dark haired.

"Well, maybe you'd be more interested if you knew what they said about *you*."

Nutty stopped. "They didn't say anything about me, Orlando. So don't start making stuff up."

"Fine. If that's what you want to believe."

"What did they say?"

"You said they didn't say anything."

"Come on, Orlando, what did they say?"

"One of them—April, I think—said that Mindy was going to be the new student council president—because she only had to beat Denton Bollander, and that would be easy. And then Carrie started saying what a good president Mindy was going to be—and stuff like that."

"Yeah? So what?"

"And then Mindy said, 'I can't be any worse than Nutty was.'"

Nutty turned and began to walk again. "I don't care. I know she thinks that."

"I thought she had the hots for you."

"She did—last summer—when she thought I was going to be a movie star. Now she can't stand me. As usual. Who cares?"

"You."

"I care what *Mindy Marshall* thinks of me? No way." But Nutty knew the truth. Maybe he didn't like Mindy, but he still hated the idea of kids saying he had been a lousy president the year before. The problem was, it was mostly true, and Nutty knew it.

"I know how we could get back at Mindy," Orlando said.

"How?"

4

"One of us could run against her for president—and beat her."

"I know. I'm thinking about running again."

"Can you do that?"

"Why not?"

"I don't know. I just thought you could only be president for one year."

"I don't think there's any rule like that."

"Why would you want to run again?"

"Because I just started catching on to things at the end of the year. I could do some good stuff now that I know what I'm doing."

They had just come to the door of the principal's office. Nutty stopped at the door.

"One thing is going be a lot better this year," Nutty said. "With Dr. Dunlop gone, it's going to be a lot easier to get things done. Dr. Kittering is pretty nice."

"Yeah. Right now. Just give her a couple of weeks."

"I don't think she'll change, Orlando. And I'm pretty sure she would like some of my ideas."

"Lay off, Nutty. You don't have *ideas*."

"See, Orlando, you're just like Mindy. You think I was a lousy president too."

"Face it, Nutty. You didn't do any of the stuff you promised."

"That's because William made me promise things that were impossible. I won't do that this time." And with that, he made up his mind. He turned and walked into the office, where he asked the secretary for a nomination form.

"This has to be in by tomorrow," the secretary told him. "And you have to get ten signatures."

"Well, that ends that," Orlando said, from behind Nutty.

Nutty turned around and said, "Why?"

"Where are you going to get ten kids who want you for president again?"

"Shut up," Nutty said. He hurried past Orlando and out the door.

But Orlando came chasing after him. "Wait up, Nutty. I was just kidding. I'll be your campaign manager."

"Are you serious?" Nutty asked.

"Yeah. We can beat Mindy—easy."

"Okay. Let's do it. Let's grab some guys and get ten names."

Orlando grinned. "Hey, little kid, come here!" he yelled. "You're going to sign this or I'm going to bust your nose, okay?"

The little boy—maybe a first-grader—looked terrified.

"Just kidding. Just kidding," Orlando said. But he made sure the kid signed his name—even if he had to print it.

Orlando and Nutty turned in the petition the next morning. Then they walked to class. They got to the room a few minutes before the bell rang, so Orlando walked over to Mindy, who was already sitting at her desk. "Gee, I'm sorry you're not going to win the election," he said.

Mindy made a face at him—an ugly, exaggerated smile.

"Oh, is that so? Do you think Denton is really going to beat me?"

"No. Nutty is."

"What?"

"He's running for reelection. We just turned the petition in."

Mindy looked shocked for maybe one full second, but then she started to laugh. "You have to be kidding," she said, looking past Orlando and straight at Nutty, who had slipped into his seat, just across from hers. "No one is going to vote for you again. You were the worst president the lab school ever had."

Nutty grinned at her. "You don't know that, Mindy," he said. "Maybe I was only the second worst. You better check the records before you start making big claims."

This seemed to throw Mindy off a little. "I don't have to check," she finally said. "I *know*."

Mr. Twitchell had been sitting at his desk, but now he stood up. "Young people, let's take our seats now," he said. "It's almost time for the bell to ring."

Mr. Twitchell was a little man—not all that short, but very thin. He wore short-sleeved shirts with bow ties, and pants that always looked a couple of sizes too big. He never stopped talking about all the reasons students should be quiet—while the kids talked.

Orlando was still grinning at Mindy. "You don't have a chance now," he said. "Every boy will vote for Nutty—and so will half the girls."

7

"No way," Mindy said. "The only reason any girl ever liked Nutty was because he was in that movie. And then the movie turned into a big mess—mostly because of him."

"And weren't you the president of his fan club, Mindy? Don't I remember you hanging around him all the time—begging for his autograph?"

"Hey, I thought it might be worth something, that's all. I didn't know he was going to turn out to be the worst actor in the history of movies."

"There you go again, Mindy," Nutty said from behind Orlando. "I may have been one of the worst actors ever. Say, in the bottom ten. But the very worst? I really doubt that."

"Shut up," Mindy told him. "You're also not funny."

"Maybe I'm not as funny as you. But I don't wear a clown nose. That gives you an advantage."

A lot of kids laughed at that one. Mindy didn't. "Just shut your mouth, okay?" she said.

But Mr. Twitchell cut the whole thing off. "That's enough," he said. "Let's all sit down. Let's be quiet during the announcements."

Orlando gave Mindy a last big grin, and then he wandered off to his seat in the back of the class.

The loudspeaker made a little popping sound, and then Dr. Kittering's smooth, controlled voice filled the room. Her first announcement was that today, Friday, was the last day for petitions for the student council presidency. And then she read off the names of the candidates nominated so far, beginning with secretary. Nutty's friend Sarah was running for vice-president against a boy named Gerald Sneddon—a real goofus.

The principal announced the three candidates for president last, and when she did, Orlando called from the back of the class, "Don't feel bad, Mindy. Maybe you'll flunk sixth grade and be able to run again next year."

Nutty laughed, and Mindy twisted in her seat and gave him a wicked smile, showing her frightening little row of shark teeth.

Actually, though, Mindy looked sort of good this year. She had let her red hair grow out a little, and she had it permed. To a guy who had never met her before, she might even have been halfway pretty, but to Nutty she was the mother of all pains in the rear. The girl had been a plague to him his whole life.

For the first time, the truth registered with Nutty. Mindy was going to be tough to run against. When she wanted something, she really went after it.

That night, when Nutty told his parents he was going to run again, his mom said, "Oh, Freddie, do you really want to do that? It was such a hassle last time."

But his dad said, "That's the spirit, Son. You're building credentials for your future."

That's when Suzie, Nutty's little sister, said, "Dad, he won't win. When the principal announced his name this morning, the kids in my class all started laughing."

"Laughing? Why?"

"Because he was such a stupid president last year. Didn't you know that?"

That brought on one of Dad's little speeches about loyalty and love in the family. It ended with, "Suzie, he's your brother."

"Hey, I can't help that," Suzie complained. "It wasn't *my* fault."

Dad's head dropped to his chest, in frustration, but Nutty wrapped his arm around Suzie. "Don't worry. I have good news," Nutty told her. "You're *not* my little sister. Mom and Dad actually found you in a garbage dumpster."

"Don't try to cheer me up," Suzie told him. She twisted out of his grasp and then slugged him hard in the stomach.

Dad started another speech, but Nutty cleared out. For one thing, he didn't want to admit that Suzie had hurt him. He was still holding his breath when he reached his bedroom.

He recovered after a minute or so, but the other blow she had delivered was still stinging. Had kids really laughed when they heard his name announced as a candidate?

Nah. That was just Suzie, exaggerating.

But Nutty wondered about it all weekend, and on Monday his worries only grew. A number of kids told him they would *never* vote for him. A couple of girls even said he was the "last person on earth" they would vote for.

Not a good sign.

But then things got worse.

Nutty was leaving school that afternoon when his friends, Charlie "Bilbo" Blackhurst and Richie Fetzer, came running up to him. Bilbo handed him a sheet of paper and said, "Have you seen this?"

Nutty read the headline across the top of the paper: Nutty Is Nuts to Run Again. What followed was a list of all the stupid things Nutty had done the year before.

"Can you believe that stuff?" Richie asked.

But Nutty was going down the list, reading the items very carefully. The problem was, he couldn't find anything on the "stupid" list that he could argue with.

Everything on it was *true!*

chapter 2

"Where did you get this?" Nutty asked Richie and Bilbo.

"Someone gave it to my little brother," Bilbo said. "But you *know* who has to be giving them out. Mindy. She and all those other girls are outside campaigning right now."

"Let's go tell her to lay off," Richie said, and he turned and marched out the door. Bilbo, who was twice the size of Richie, took two steps and caught up. And Nutty followed— lagging well behind. He wasn't too eager to discuss any of the items on the list.

"Hey, Mindy," Richie was yelling, "you better quit handing out these sheets!"

"What sheets?" she said.

"You *know* what sheets. These fliers you've been giving people."

She took the paper from Richie and looked at it. And she

really did seem surprised. "I've never even seen this before," she said. But she smiled as she began to read it.

"Don't put on such an act," Bilbo said. "You're the only one who would hand out something like that."

But Mindy didn't respond. She was too busy reading the rest of the list. And her friends, including Sarah Montag, gathered around to look over her shoulder.

"We didn't write this stuff," Carrie said immediately. But the denial came a little too fast. Nutty didn't think she had even had time to look at it.

Sarah said, "Really, Nutty. We didn't do this."

And for a moment Nutty believed her. But then he saw the button that all the girls, *including* Sarah, were wearing. It said: Mindy Is NOT Nutty.

"Yeah, right," Nutty said.

At the same moment, Sarah seemed to realize what Nutty was looking at. She turned red instantly. True, Sarah, with her light skin, blushed easily, but she suddenly looked awfully guilty.

"We didn't write it, but all those things are true," Mindy said.

"No way," Richie told her. "It's all lies. Nothing but lie after lie after lie."

By now, a lot of kids had come over to see what was going on. Nutty could see that Mindy had a sack full of the buttons, and the girls had been handing them out. Some of the kids who came over were already wearing them.

13

"The first one is true!" April shouted at Richie. "Last year Nutty promised he was going to get longer recesses for us—and he never did."

"That wasn't his fault," Richie told her. "Dunlop wouldn't do it. But Nutty's going to get it done this year."

"Oh, right? Is that what you're promising now?" April asked Nutty.

Nutty knew better than to start making big claims. He hesitated, not sure what to say.

"*Seeeeeee.* He won't answer that."

"Look at the second one!" Mindy screeched. "He said he was going to get better food in the cafeteria, and that never happened either."

"He *tried,*" Bilbo said.

"Oh, he tried. Should we re-elect him because he tried?"

"Hey, this year we've got a new principal," Bilbo said. "Nutty can get some stuff done this time." This wasn't really like Bilbo to get so wound up. He spent his life reading—and was usually quiet. But he was a loyal friend. Nutty appreciated that.

"How do we know he'll even go to the student council meetings?" Mindy demanded to know. "It says right here that he forgot to go three different times last year."

"That's the biggest lie there!" Richie screamed into Mindy's face. But then he turned to Nutty. "Isn't it?"

Nutty glanced away and shrugged just a little. The only thing he really wanted to say was, "Richie, keep your mouth shut," but he knew better than to say that.

His silence was a great triumph for the girls, however. They all started laughing and saying, "See. See. He can't even deny it."

About thirty kids were standing around Nutty now, and all of them were watching him. Most of them were laughing—even the boys. Only Richie and Bilbo seemed to be on his side.

"You did forget about some of the meetings, didn't you?" Mindy asked again.

Nutty heard a voice behind him whisper, "Don't answer, Nutty. Let's get out of here."

It was Orlando.

Nutty turned to walk away, but that got the biggest laugh yet. Suddenly Nutty turned back and said, "Yes."

"Yes . . . what?"

"I missed some meetings."

"Three?"

"I don't know," Nutty said, softly. "Three or four. I don't remember."

"Be quiet. Don't admit *anything*," Orlando said more loudly this time.

"*Four!*" Carrie shouted. "He admits to four."

"He said 'maybe,'" Richie said, but he was not shouting now. He was backing away.

Nutty thought about admitting to the whole thing. He had been a pretty lousy president, and the stuff on the sheet was true. Everyone knew that. But that didn't mean he would do things the same way if he got elected again.

Orlando grabbed Nutty's arm and pulled. "Come on, Nutty," he said. "Don't say anything else."

"Yeah, Nutty," Mindy said. "You better keep your mouth shut. You only make things worse for yourself when you start talking."

Nutty couldn't resist. He patted Mindy on the shoulder and said, "I think I might vote for you, Mindy."

"Oh, yeah. I'm sure."

"No, really. You keep saying I was the worst president ever. But if you were president for a year, I'm sure you could replace me at the bottom of the list."

"Oh, is that right? Well, you're right about one thing. You are the *bottom*."

"Well, you're a bottom."

"And you're a *butthead*."

"Yeah? Well, why don't you paint a face on your fanny and walk around backward? You'd look better."

Suddenly Mindy was coming after him.

But Orlando jumped between them. "Hey, that's enough, you two!" he shouted.

Mindy tried to fight her way around Orlando, but he clung to her, and then her friends pulled her back.

Nutty was already mad at himself for letting Mindy get him so mad. She had only made him look bad.

Orlando was obviously thinking the same thing. "Now listen, everybody!" he yelled. "Nutty's campaign hasn't started yet—not officially. But tomorrow we'll have some

16

very exciting announcements. Nutty has some great things planned."

"So what's he promising this year?" Mindy shouted. "What's he going to *try* to do?"

"Don't answer," Orlando commanded.

But Nutty couldn't resist saying, "I want to do some things to make sure we get a good education around here."

For a moment Nutty thought Mindy was going to fall over backward. "Oh, right," she gasped. "That's something you have always cared a lot about. You're such a *serious* student."

"I didn't say anything about being serious."

But now Orlando had hold of one arm and Richie the other. And Nutty was leaving—whether his feet knew it or not.

All the girls were laughing again, and the boys probably were too. Nutty felt like telling them all to jump off the planet. He did have some things he wanted to accomplish, whether they believed him or not.

"Come on. We need to go see William," Orlando said. "We're in trouble. We need *help*."

Nutty twisted loose from his friends. "Don't pull me," he said. "I can walk on my own."

"Well, you can't *talk* on your own. What were you thinking about? You can't say stuff like that."

"Okay. Okay. But Mindy drives me crazy."

"Nutty, you admitted to too many things. If you're going

to go around telling everyone the truth, you might as well drop out right now."

Nutty rolled his eyes, and Bilbo laughed. But Orlando didn't see any humor in what he had said.

Nutty was about to tell Orlando he was going to do things his own way this time. But then he heard a voice from behind them.

"Nutty. Wait a minute."

Nutty knew the voice, and he was surprised. It was Sarah.

He turned to look at her, and she motioned to him. "Come here a sec," she said. "I need to talk to you."

"Don't you mean *me*, Sarah?" Orlando said. "I'm better looking than Nutty."

She didn't answer. But she looked embarrassed.

Nutty walked over to her while his friends waited.

"I'm sorry," Sarah told Nutty.

"Sorry for what? Did you guys write that stuff?"

"No, we didn't."

"I'll bet Mindy did."

"I don't think so. Really. At least she never said anything to me about it."

"I still think she wrote it."

Sarah was looking good. She seemed a little worried, still a little flushed in the cheeks. And her eyes looked very blue. That made for a lot of very nice pink and blue, and her new short haircut looked sort of . . . *pert,* like the ads on TV always said. Best of all, she had taken the campaign button off.

"I'm sorry I was wearing that button. I told the girls I didn't want to do any negative stuff about you, and they all started teasing me. So I put it on. But I didn't want to."

"But you want her to win?"

"Well . . . she's my friend and everything."

"You don't *like* her, do you, Sarah? The only reason she's running is so she can be a big shot."

"I know."

Nutty waited. He couldn't believe kids would really vote for Mindy.

"I'm running for vice-president. If I don't campaign for her, she won't campaign for me."

"You don't need her. Just run by yourself."

"All my friends are working together—for both of us."

Nutty shrugged. "Well . . . whatever. It doesn't matter."

"Nutty, why did you admit you missed those meetings?"

"Because I did."

"I know. But Mindy will just use that against you. Didn't you do some good things?"

"Yeah."

"Well, tell about that. That's what you have to do if you want to win."

"Why?"

"I don't know. That's just what you do."

"Kids know I wasn't very good. I might as well just admit it."

"Nutty, you're going to get *murdered* if you say stuff like that. And then Mindy will win."

"Well, that's what you want. So you'll be happy."

Sarah gave a little shake of her head. Nutty wasn't certain whether that meant that she didn't want Mindy to win, or whether she was just frustrated with Nutty. In either case, she said, "See you later. Mindy's going to be mad at me for talking to you."

She walked a few steps away, but then she stopped and looked back. "Good luck," she said. And she smiled.

It was one of those make-a-guy-feel-weak-in-the-knees sort of smiles. But Nutty acted as though he hardly noticed it. He nodded and said, "Thanks."

Then Sarah hurried off to her friends. Nutty was left wondering what she was really thinking. When he walked back to his own friends, Orlando was grinning. "Hey, I thought she dumped you. Does she want to go with you again or something?"

"We didn't ever *go* together, Orlando. We're just friends."

"Yeah, right."

"Hey, it's true."

"Well, I'll tell you what I think. Those girls don't really like Mindy. They may hang around with her—but they won't vote for her when it comes right down to it. That's why we still have a chance. Denton is a nerd. And Mindy is . . . Mindy. If you can't beat those two, you're a disaster."

"Maybe that's what I am."

"Well, true. But you're still better than those two."

"Oh . . . thanks a lot."

"Nutty, I think you're in trouble," Bilbo said. "Maybe we

better go talk to William Bilks. Maybe he'll know what we can do."

"Hey, I'm Nutty's campaign manager this time," Orlando said.

"Then he's *really* in trouble," Richie said.

"Shut up. I know what I'm doing."

Nutty thought for a moment, and then he said, "Bilbo's right. We better go see William."

chapter 3

William, who attended a private school, was always a little later getting home than Nutty and the other boys. When Nutty had finally reached him on the telephone, William had said he would come over to Nutty's house for a meeting, but he couldn't stay long. He was taking a class at the university that night.

William Bilks, needless to say, was not an *average* twelve-year-old.

He was now sitting on the floor in Nutty's bedroom. His legs were crossed under him—like a yoga master—and his plump little fingers were laced together. He thought for a time, and finally he pronounced his decision.

"Nutty, I think you should withdraw. You have little chance of winning, and the whole thing isn't that important anyway."

"Are you sure?" Orlando said. "I know Nutty isn't much of a candidate, but isn't there some way we could get him elected?"

"It's highly unlikely, Orlando."

"Just because he was so bad last year?"

"It's not just that," William said. "We tried to improve his image during the last campaign. But the general impression most students have now is that he's quite undependable." William stopped, seemed to think for a moment, and then he chuckled to himself. "Of course, that's because he's really *not* very dependable."

All of Nutty's great buddies had a good laugh about that.

Bilbo, Orlando, and Richie were lined up on the floor, leaning against Nutty's bed. Their bare legs were all sticking out from the shorts they were wearing—but Bilbo's stuck out twice as far as the others'.

Nutty was on that same bed, behind his friends. He had been lying on his side, listening to William, but now he rolled onto his back. He felt as though he were attending his own funeral—except no one was saying what a great guy he had been.

"Well, I guess that's that," Orlando said. "Mindy will be a stupid president—but it doesn't make that much difference, I guess."

"That's exactly right," William told him. He pushed his glasses up with one finger, and he looked very satisfied with himself. "The world will go on . . . somehow."

The meeting was over, and Nutty's friends were all getting up from the floor. But then Nutty said, "I'm not dropping out. I'm staying in the race."

Everyone turned to look at him. "Why?" Richie asked him.

"There's some stuff I want to do."

"Oh, brother," Orlando said. "Nutty, what you want to do and what you *can* do are two different things."

"That's okay. I'm still going to try."

Everyone was staring at Nutty, obviously convinced that he had lost his mind.

Nutty didn't care. "Maybe I can get everybody to forget last year," he said. "I'll just tell them I have a good plan for the future."

"Nutty, kids don't vote because of stuff like that," Orlando said. "Maybe grown-ups do—but kids don't care about *plans* for the *future*."

"You're wrong there," William said.

Nutty rolled onto his side again and took a better look at William. He sounded as though he were coming over to Nutty's side.

But William said, "I'm not saying that kids care about those things. I'm merely saying that adults don't either. They vote for silly reasons, the same as you do. They like someone's style, a glittering smile—those kinds of things."

"Why do they do that?" Nutty asked.

William stepped closer to the bed and looked down at Nutty. "Most issues are simply too complicated for people to understand. That's all."

"So what are you saying—that people are stupid?"

"Well . . . they aren't so much stupid as they are confused by the heavy load of information that's coming at them. So they latch on to some simple slogan. 'This guy will put you back to work.' Or, 'This woman stands up for common people.' It's easier to repeat something like that than it is to think."

"Okay. I've got a good slogan," Nutty said.

"And what's that, Nutty?"

All the boys were standing around Nutty's bed now, still looking down at him, as though he were a body in a coffin.

"I messed up last year, but next year I'll do a better job."

William was obviously amused by that. He chuckled in his grandfatherly style. "Well, now, that *is* a fresh approach," he said. "No politician ever tried that one."

But Orlando said, "It's stupid. Isn't it, William?"

"Yes. Of course. But I still rather like it."

"Answer me this, William," Richie said. "Is there *any way* that Nutty could win now?"

"Well, politicians can make amazing comebacks—with the right sort of campaign. Surely it's possible—just not very likely."

"What would we have to do so that he could beat Mindy?"

"Probably pin some negative labels on her so that she looks as bad as he does."

"You mean, call her names?" Richie said.

William held his head to one side, looking wise. "Well,

that's not a delicate way to say it. But yes. You could spread the word that she's . . . I don't know . . . a . . ."

"An *airhead!*" Bilbo said.

"Yes. That's good. And it's quite an accurate picture of the girl too." William crossed his arms over his little gray sweater. "If you could bring her down to Nutty's level, then you would have a fighting chance."

"Okay, but if we say she's an airhead, and Mindy says Nutty is a big mess-up, who wins?"

"One danger is that the whole thing could be thrown to Denton. He isn't strong, but he's not objectionable either. You may have to label Denton with some negative term of his own."

"He's a wimp," Richie said.

"There you go. That's just the thing. No one wants a weakling for a leader."

Nutty sat up. "So everyone throws a lot of mud at everybody else—and no one says what we plan to do if we get elected," Nutty said. "Does that make any sense?"

"Nutty, I consider the state of politics absolutely disgraceful. I don't approve of any of it. But Richie asked how you could win, and I'm telling you how the game is played. Politicians make lots of broad, general promises. And then they spend their time attaching negative images to their opponents. It's ugly, but it works."

"I won't do it," Nutty said, and he flopped back onto his bed.

"I don't blame you," William said. "I told you in the beginning, you should drop from the race."

"I'm not doing that either."

Orlando leaned over Nutty, so he was looking straight into his face. "Fine. Then you're on your own. You tell people, 'I messed up last year, but I'll do better this time,' or whatever it was, and we'll all vote for Denton—just so Mindy won't win."

"That's okay. Go ahead."

"Come on, Nutty," Bilbo said. "If you keep this up, Mindy *will* win. If you don't care about being president that's up to you. But I'd like to find some way to beat Mindy."

"Of course, Nutty's instincts could be right," William said. "Maybe the honest approach is worth trying. Maybe young people are looking for a leader who can accept blame for his own mistakes and who can forge ahead with a new vision. Maybe it's time for a bold new approach to politics."

"Do you really think so?" Nutty asked, beginning to sit up again.

William laughed. "No. Of course not. But it couldn't hurt anything to try. You'll probably lose no matter what you do."

Nutty thought for a few seconds, and then he slid off his bed, stepped to the middle of the room, and pointed to the door. "Okay. Everybody get out of here."

"Oh, thanks a lot," Orlando said. "We came over here to help you."

"Yeah, and all you've talked about is what a lousy candidate I am. So don't waste your time. I'll run my own campaign."

"What are you going to do?" Richie asked him.

"I'm not saying anything bad about anybody. Our school needs some changes, and I have some ideas about stuff we could do. I'm just going to tell people that. And if I lose, I lose."

"That's the right attitude to take, Nutty," William said.

"Thanks, William." Nutty felt a little better.

"Well, I only mean that you *will* lose, so it's good to be prepared."

The boys all laughed at that one.

But Nutty didn't. He sat down on his bed. "Okay. I'll see you guys later," he said.

But Richie must have felt sorry for him. He said, "Hey, Nutty, I'll still help you."

"Yeah. I will too," Bilbo said.

"Now that's what I call loyalty," William said. "These young men admire your principles. They're willing to stay with the ship—even when it's taking on water and about to go down."

He and Orlando had another good laugh.

But then Orlando said, "Look, I'll stay with you too. I'll still be your campaign manager. We'll go down fighting— bailing water all the way down."

Nutty could have lived without the cute remarks, but he was still pleased that his friends were willing to stick with him.

"Here's what I suggest," William said. "Let Nutty plan his own campaign. Let him do it his way. The rest of us will merely back him up where we can."

"Okay," Nutty said. "That's fine with me. You guys can go. I need to think about all this."

So everyone left.

And Nutty tried to think. But at that point reality began to set in. Losing to *Mindy* was going to be hard to take. And talking to kids about making changes at the school—educational changes—was not going to be easy.

The thought crossed his mind that Mindy was an airhead, and maybe it really wasn't so bad to call her that.

But he said out loud, "*No!* I won't do that."

His little sister was across the hall in her room and both bedroom doors were open. She suddenly appeared at his door. "What did you say, Nutty?"

"Nothing."

"Have you started talking to yourself or something?"

"Get lost."

"I mean, I know you're stupid, but I didn't know you were crazy too."

"Shut up, Suzie."

"Nutty, I heard some of that stuff those guys were telling you."

"Then you were listening with your ear to the door."

"How did you know?"

"Because you do it all the time."

"How did you know that?"

"Because I can hear the wind blow through your ears, Suzie. What do you mean, how do I know?"

"Shut up, Nutty. I'm not an *airhead.* I'm not like Mindy."

"So you don't like Mindy either?"

"Nobody likes Mindy. Mindy's best friends don't like Mindy."

"So maybe she can't beat me."

"Are you serious?"

"Yeah, I am."

"Nutty, you don't know what kids are saying. They don't like Mindy. And they gag at the idea of Denton being president. But they all say you're the worst of the three. Most kids don't want to vote for *any* of you."

"Will you vote for me?"

It was not a good question. It was handing Suzie a perfect opportunity. And it was something Nutty never would have done if he hadn't been so discouraged. But right now he almost wanted one more insult, just to feel a little lousier.

Suzie must have felt that, and Nutty was apparently too far down for even her to give him one more kick. "Yeah, I'll vote for you," she said.

"Thanks."

"But it's only because I'm your sister. And, you know, two votes—mine and yours—aren't going to do it."

"Don't you think *anyone* else will vote for me?"

Suzie thought for a time. "There's a new girl in my class

this year. Maybe I could talk her into it. She doesn't know you."

"Thanks a lot."

"Hey, I'm not a miracle worker. It's the best I can do." Suzie walked back to her room.

Nutty stretched out on his bed and clutched his hands across his chest.

"Just go ahead and bury me," he told the universe.

chapter *4*

The next morning Nutty still felt crummy. And then he decided he was going to take a new attitude. "I don't care what William says," he told himself. "I'm going to tell the truth. And I'm going to *win*."

He liked the way he felt. It was him against the world, and he liked the odds.

And then he went to school.

Orlando met him in the hallway and handed him another flier. "Look what they're spreading about you today," he said.

Nutty took the flier and read the headline: Nutty Is a Loser!

Nutty didn't care about that. But he began to read, and the information in the flier was pretty hard to take. The first paragraph read:

A lot of people think that Nutty Nutsell gave up acting

because he didn't like it. The truth is, he was a terrible actor. He knew it, and so did anyone who ever watched him. Poor Sarah Montag had to put up with his horrible acting and suffer through lots of disgusting kisses besides. She told everyone she never wanted to kiss the guy again. So Nutty lost his movie part and his girlfriend. What a loser!

Nutty was the first to admit he was a lousy actor. But the part about Sarah was only about half true, and even at that, it was rotten stuff to be spreading around.

But it was the next paragraph that really bugged him:

Some people know that Nutty and his friend William Bilks once tried an experiment with light rays for a science project. And a lot of kids know that Nutty ended up with his head glowing in the dark! What people don't know is that while the light rays were around his head, he only told the truth. It was during that time that he told Mindy Marshall that he loved her! She, of course, was disgusted by the very idea—and she told him to get lost. He's been feeling bad about that ever since. Now he wants to take something away from Mindy—since she once rejected him. So make him a loser one more time. It's what he deserves.

By the time Nutty finished, he was *mad*. "What *junk*," he said. "It's a bunch of . . . well, it's not exactly lies. But it's not really true either."

"This stuff has to be coming from either Sarah or Mindy," Orlando said. "They're the ones who knew about those things."

33

"Not Sarah. It sounds like Mindy."

"I think they're both involved. They're doing all their campaigning together."

But Nutty still refused to believe Sarah would be in on it. "Do you think kids will believe all that stuff?"

"I don't know, Nutty," Orlando said. "I hope not."

He and Nutty were standing in the hallway, which was starting to fill up as lots of kids were showing up for school.

A sixth-grade boy named Jeremy Tredway stopped next to them. He pointed to the flier in Nutty's hand. "Hey, Nutty, that stuff is all lies, isn't it?" he said. "You never told Mindy you *loved* her."

Nutty hesitated. He needed to explain the whole thing, which was really pretty complicated. "It's mostly lies," he finally said.

"What do you mean . . . 'mostly'?"

"Well, I did say that to Mindy. But I didn't mean it that way. You have to understand what those light rays did to me. It wasn't like . . . you know . . . love. Not the way . . ."

Jeremy was giving Nutty a very strange look. "That's *sick*," he said, and he walked away.

Orlando told Nutty, "Don't be so stupid. Just say, 'No. I never said it.'"

"But I did."

"Oh, brother." Orlando shook his head. "You're doing it *your* way, all right. You're telling the truth and giving the *wrong* impression."

That was true. But Nutty didn't know what to do. He had

told himself over and over that he was going to stay above all the ugly politics—all the lying and accusing—and do things right.

"Maybe if Mindy keeps writing stuff like this, and I keep telling the truth, people will get sick of her and vote for me."

"Yeah, right. And maybe your fairy godmother will step in and save the day. Or a truck will run over Mindy. Lots of *wonderful* things might happen."

"Look, Mindy is lying. She writes this stuff and then says she doesn't. That's *got* to look bad for her."

"Maybe kids believe her."

"Do you think so?"

"Well, the ones who are on her side probably do."

"I wish we could *prove* she was writing them."

"How could we do that?"

"Maybe we could follow her. She must be taking them to a copy place to get them printed up."

"Maybe not. Maybe she writes the stuff on a computer and then just prints a whole bunch of them."

That was true. But there must be some way to prove it.

About then Nutty heard some girls giggling. "Hey, Nutty, we just read some *very interesting* things about you."

Orlando spun around and said, "It's all lies."

But the four fourth-grade girls were still giggling. "Hey," Nutty said, "I *was* a terrible actor. I know that. But I never was 'in love' with Mindy. Just ask her who was the president of my fan club last summer—because *she* was. She was the one who liked me—not the other way around."

"Oh, sure," one of them said, and they all laughed again.

"Hey, that's the truth," Orlando said.

But the girls were still laughing as they walked away. And Nutty found that frustrating.

Suddenly he wanted to confront Mindy. He walked down the hallway to the classroom. When he got there, he saw her perched at her desk like a little dove of peace. He wanted to sock her one in the beak.

"Mindy, I can't believe how rotten you're being," he said. "Where do you get off writing all this stuff about me?" He held the flier in front of her nose.

She glared at him. "Nutty, I already told you—I'm not writing those fliers. The one this morning was *embarrassing*. Do you think I want people to know what you said to me? It's the worst memory of my whole life."

"Yeah, right. You're the *only* one who could have written this and you know it."

Mindy started another denial, but Mr. Twitchell told Nutty to sit down and get ready for class to start.

So Nutty sat down. But he was thinking *hard*. Somehow he had to show Mindy for what she really was. How could he prove that she was the one writing the fliers?

All day he wondered. Maybe he could prove that the print had come from her computer printer. But he didn't know how to get a sample from her printer.

Someone must be handing the fliers out for her. Orlando said he had found them on the floor. But someone had put them there. Nutty needed to trace the sheets back to Mindy. He needed to *stake her out*—follow her every minute.

At lunch, Nutty told Orlando, "We need to catch her putting them in the hallway—or giving them to someone. And maybe get a picture of her."

"That's going to be tough to do," Orlando told him.

"Maybe so. But we have to try. Will you go with me after school and help me watch her house?"

"Yeah. I guess. But I don't think it'll do any good."

All the same, after school Nutty gathered up Richie and Bilbo, along with Orlando, and the four got ready to follow Mindy home.

The only problem was, they had to sit on the front lawn of the school and watch the girls campaign. Mindy and Sarah and their friends were handing out more buttons again, but these were not about Nutty. They read: Mindy and Sarah for a Better School.

When the girls finally left the school, the boys followed at a considerable distance, and they stayed behind hedges and houses, corners and trees, trying not to be spotted.

All the girls stopped at Mindy's house, and they talked for a time, but then they split up and went their separate ways. Mindy went into her house.

"So what do we do now?" Bilbo asked.

"Let's move in a little closer and then keep watch," Nutty said.

"What if she doesn't go anywhere?"

"We'll just keep waiting."

"Hey, Nutty, I'm sorry, but I've got better things to do," Bilbo said.

"All you're going to do is go home and read a book, Bilbo."

"That's right. I've got better things to do."

"Me too," Richie said. "I want to help with your campaign, but this is pointless."

"Will you stay, Orlando?" Nutty asked.

"I don't know, Nutty. Yeah. For a while."

So Bilbo and Richie left but Orlando stayed. He and Nutty hid across the street from Mindy's house, down a little alley and behind a little shed. Nutty did leave long enough to go home for his camera, and then the boys took turns going home long enough to eat dinner, but they never let up on the watch.

And nothing happened.

They never once saw Mindy. And now it was getting dark.

Orlando had begun to complain that he had had enough when Nutty said, "Wait a minute. Who's that?"

Mindy lived in a big, white two-story house with an old-fashioned screened porch. Two girls had just turned up her front walk and were now stepping onto the porch. They rang the doorbell. In a second or two, the porch light came on.

"It's Sarah," Orlando said. "Sarah and Carrie."

Nutty had already seen that. "Okay. The action is beginning," he said.

"What action?"

"They're probably going to work on the next flier together." But he actually hated to think that Sarah was in on it.

In a few seconds, a light came on upstairs. "That must be Mindy's room," Nutty said.

"Nutty, I'm not going to wait for a long time. If Carrie and Sarah leave after a while, we won't know whether they have the fliers or whether Mindy does. Or whether they even did any."

Nutty had already gotten that far. "That's right. So let's go climb that big tree. We can see right into her room that way. And we'll know what they're doing."

"So what? We can't get a picture from there. How could we prove anything?"

"At least we'll know."

"No way, Nutty."

"Why not?"

"We could get caught."

"We'll be careful. Come on."

So Nutty crept down the alley and then dashed across the street to the tree. Orlando followed.

But the first limb on the big maple tree was quite high. Nutty jumped but couldn't grab it.

"Boost me up," Orlando said. "Then I'll pull you up."

So Nutty gave Orlando a leg up, and Orlando reached down and helped Nutty. They struggled, but Nutty finally got his arm around the limb and then Orlando climbed to a higher branch and got out of Nutty's way.

The going after that was easy. Orlando worked his way up through the branches ahead of Nutty until he announced that he could see into the room.

Nutty tried to worm his way up next to Orlando, but Orlando said, "Be careful, Nutty. There's not enough room on this limb."

"Okay, okay. Can you see them?"

"Yeah."

"What are they doing?"

At that moment Nutty heard a distant siren, and he froze. Orlando said, "Oh, no. They're looking out the window. They must have heard us or something. We better get out of here."

Nutty panicked.

He scrambled down through the limbs, almost wildly, and dropped from the bottom limb. "Hurry, Orlando," he whispered.

The siren was coming closer.

Orlando seemed incredibly slow, but he finally plopped down on the ground next to Nutty, and Nutty grabbed him and pulled. "Over the back fence!" he whispered, and the two dashed into the backyard.

Nutty leaped onto the fence and was over almost in one motion. But Orlando was much shorter. He jumped and grabbed the top of the fence and then had to struggle to get over.

The siren was not far away now.

"Hurry, Orlando! Hurry!"

40

Orlando made it over as the siren screamed its way up the street.

"Back here!" Nutty whispered, and the two ran down the little alley behind the back fence. They dodged into some high weeds alongside a garage, and they ducked down.

Nutty was breathing hard. Would the police come looking? Would they start driving around the neighborhood? Was it better to sit tight or to run for it down the alley?

And then he realized. The siren had kept right on going.

Orlando noticed at the same time. "It's going away," he said. "I think it was an ambulance or something. It wasn't even after us."

Nutty stood up, greatly relieved.

"Let's get out of here," Orlando said.

"Why? They weren't after us. We can climb the tree again."

"No. The girls were looking out."

"Maybe they just heard the siren."

"I don't think so."

"Why not?"

"They were looking at the tree, I think."

"Maybe. But I don't think they could see us. Let's give them some time. And then we'll climb the tree again."

"We don't need to, Nutty. I saw what they were doing. Mindy was sitting at her computer, typing away like mad. And the girls were sitting there telling her things to write."

"Even Sarah?"

"Yup."

Nutty was pulling burrs from his T-shirt, and then he bent to pull some from the bottom of his jeans. "Okay," he said, "but how can we prove it?"

"I don't know. But I'm not going back up that tree."

"Since when did you get so chicken? We've done lots of stuff like that before."

"I just don't want to get caught. My parents would throw a fit. Besides, I've got homework to do."

Nutty admitted to himself that he had work to do too.

"Maybe if we just wait until they leave, we can—"

"Come on, Nutty, we can't hang around here all night. They could be in there a long time."

Nutty had to admit that was true.

So the boys gave it up and went home. Nutty wasn't at all satisfied though. He had found out what he had suspected. But that wouldn't do one bit of good if he couldn't prove it.

chapter 5

Nutty had hardly walked through the door of the school the next morning when kids started sticking the latest flier in his face.

But this one was stunning.

The headline was: Nutty Nutsell Is a Window Peeker. And the story was to the point. It simply said:

Last night Nutty Nutsell climbed a tree next to Mindy Marshall's house and tried to peek into Mindy's bedroom window. When Nutty heard sirens, he quickly climbed out of the tree and ran. He was not caught by the police, but witnesses saw him in the tree looking into Mindy's window.

"They're lying, aren't they?" a kid was asking Nutty.

"Who is?"

"Those girls."

"I don't know," Nutty mumbled, and he walked away.

But what he meant was that he didn't know whether it was the girls or someone else who was behind this one.

He got almost to class before he realized he didn't want to go in and face Mindy and the other girls. So he waited outside, and he tried to think. What was going on? Who could have known this?

But waiting outside was a mistake. Mindy was not inside. She came up behind him and dug her claws into his shoulder.

Nutty spun around and saw that Mindy had the flier in her hand. "You were peeking in my *window?*" she screamed. "I can't believe this."

"Hey, I didn't . . . I mean . . . I wasn't trying to . . ." But Nutty didn't know what to say. Anything would sound wrong.

"You are scum, Nutty. I always thought you were just stupid. It turns out you're a . . . *window peeker*. That's disgusting."

"It's not like you think."

"You admit it, don't you?"

"Not that I was window peeking. I was only trying to see if you girls were writing those fliers. And you *were*. So don't act so innocent."

The kids inside the classroom—and some coming down the hall—heard the ruckus. And they all started gathering around Nutty and Mindy.

Mindy told them, "Read this. He was peeking in my window last night. And he *admits* it."

"It was like spying," Nutty said. "We were trying to find out if she was doing these fliers. Carrie and April and Sarah were there too."

Orlando was suddenly next to Nutty, whispering desperately, "Don't say another word, Nutty. You're only making things worse."

But Carrie was saying, "You're *sick*, Nutty. Re*volt*ing."

And Sarah was staring at him, looking shocked and disappointed.

Nutty couldn't think of one thing to do or say.

"We were making posters," Mindy said. "We weren't writing fliers. We don't have to say bad things about you, Nutty. You do too many *stupid* things on your own."

Nutty saw Sarah nod her agreement. And suddenly he felt like the biggest jerk in the world. But she had the wrong idea. Entirely.

When the bell rang, everyone went into class and sat down. But the girls kept whispering during the announcements—and then looking over at him.

Nutty stared straight ahead. But his mind was working, and he was pretty sure now that a traitor was selling him out. He just couldn't think who it could be.

When recess came, Nutty grabbed his friends and got as far away from everyone else as he could get. The four boys hurried to the corner of the playground.

"Okay, something is going on here," Nutty said. "I didn't tell *anybody* about what happened last night."

"They must have seen us," Orlando told him.

"Remember how they were looking out the window?"

"You were the one they would have seen. You were higher up in the tree than I was."

"Maybe they saw somebody and figured it must be you."

"Or maybe they saw you when you jumped out of the tree," Bilbo said.

"How do you know what happened?" Nutty asked him.

"Orlando called me last night. He told me all about it."

"Did *you* tell anyone?"

"No. Just Richie."

"Richie, did you say anything?"

"No. The only person I told was Andy Folkman, and I told him not to tell anyone."

"That's how it got out," Orlando said. "Folkman has a big mouth. From now on, Richie, if we have secrets, we can't allow any leaks. We have to keep everything *tight*."

"Orlando, what are you talking about?" Nutty said. "How could it have gotten back to those girls that fast?"

But Bilbo said, "All Folkman had to do was say something to the wrong person, and someone could have called Mindy. She could have typed it into her computer in a couple of minutes."

"I'm sorry," Richie said. "I really didn't think Andy would say anything."

Nutty thought about all that. He supposed Richie had been the leak, and he probably hadn't meant any harm. He was not the sort of guy who would try to help Mindy. "Well, whatever happened," he said, "I'm ruined. Everyone in the school thinks I'm a window peeker."

"Yeah, but that's only because you tried to peek in a window," Bilbo said. "And that wasn't very smart."

"Come on, Bilbo," Orlando said. "It wasn't window peeking. We were just trying to prove what Mindy was doing."

"It was still stupid," Bilbo said.

But all that didn't matter now. The damage was done. And Nutty had no idea what to do about it.

He was still thinking about it, though, when he saw Denton Bollander walking toward him. As Denton walked up, he said, "Nutty, I don't like those sheets that Mindy has been handing out. She has no right to do that kind of stuff."

Denton was a nice guy and all that, but he was sort of nerdy, and worst of all, in Nutty's opinion, he used that mousse stuff to comb his hair. But for the first time, Nutty had another thought about him. And Orlando was apparently thinking the same thing. "How do we know *you* aren't the one doing the fliers?"

"Because I wouldn't do something like that."

"Why not? If you could get Nutty to quit, you might pick up the boys' vote."

"Orlando, how would I know any of that stuff? I don't know if he was looking in Mindy's window or not."

"The word got around last night. We know that. We

thought maybe it got to Mindy, but it's a lot more likely that it got to you, now that I think about it."

Orlando had a point. "Did Andy Folkman talk to you last night?" Nutty asked.

"Nope. I hardly ever talk to Folkman. Why?"

"What kind of printer do you have on your computer?" Orlando asked him.

"Why?"

"Do you have a laser printer?"

"No."

"I'll bet your dad does—at his office."

"Sure. But I don't use it."

"You *could.*"

"Look, I didn't write that stuff. Honest."

Yeah, maybe. Nutty didn't know what to believe anymore.

On the way back to class after recess, Nutty got a lot of teasing from just about everyone. He acted as though he didn't hear it. But when he got back to the room, Mr. Twitchell told him that the principal wanted to see him.

That he did hear.

And so he took the long walk down the hall. He hoped he would have to wait for a while, but the secretary told him to go right on into Dr. Kittering's office.

When he got there, he was expecting the Dr. Dunlop stare he had gotten so many times the year before. But Dr. Kittering smiled. She was a young woman, maybe in her thirties, and even sort of pretty, if Nutty could have forgotten that she was the principal. But she also looked very businesslike.

"Sit down, Frederick," she said. "My secretary showed me this flier that someone is handing around. Do you know anything about it?"

"I think Mindy Marshall is handing them out, but I'm not sure. This is the third one."

"What did the other two say?"

"One said I was a lousy president last year, and the other one said I was a big loser."

"Have you seen who is handing them out?"

"No."

"So you have no proof that Mindy is the one who wrote them?"

Dr. Kittering sounded a little like the lawyers Nutty had heard on TV. Her tone made him nervous. "No," he said. "But she would do it. She hates me."

"Does she hate you enough to tell lies about you?"

"Well . . . I didn't say they were lies, exactly."

"Excuse me?"

"I really wasn't a very good president last year. And the loser stuff was sort of true, in a way."

Dr. Kittering actually smiled, even though she was obviously trying not to. "But what about this window-peeking incident?"

"Okay, that happened. But it wasn't like she made it sound. See, she keeps saying that she isn't writing the fliers. So I wanted to catch her at it. I saw her friends show up at her house, and I thought I could climb the tree and spot them writing that stuff."

Dr. Kittering leaned back in her chair. She laced her fingers together and considered for a time. Her nails were polished, red, and they were quite long. "Climbing that tree and looking in the window was a very bad decision," she finally said.

"I know."

"I don't like these fliers, Frederick. I'm going to talk to Mindy and Denton. I'll try to get to the bottom of this."

"Good."

"But number one, I don't want you producing anything of this sort. And number two, this spying stuff has got to stop."

"Okay."

Nutty thought he was finished, and overall, he was glad things had gone so well. But then Dr. Kittering asked him something he didn't expect. "What makes you want to run again if you admit you didn't do very well last year?"

"I have some plans. You know, to make the school better."

"What, for instance?"

"Well, here's what I've been thinking." Nutty had been scrunching down in his chair, ready for any attack that might come his way, but now he sat up straight. "Teachers tell us what we need to learn, and they give us assignments and everything. But I think kids should be allowed to give their opinions about what we want to learn."

"And what do you think students want to learn that we're not teaching?"

"Okay, here's something I thought about. What if we let kids submit questions—you know, things they're curious about. Like, I've always wondered what makes a curveball curve. I think I'd really listen to the answer—and remember it. And learn something about . . ."

"The laws of physics."

"Yeah."

"What you're proposing is a very old philosophy of education. The theory is that people only learn—and remember—what they feel a need to know."

"Oh." Nutty had no idea he had hit on a "philosophy of education." But it sounded good.

"The problem is, we can't wait until children feel the need to know arithmetic before we teach it to them."

"Yeah. I know. But if kids got to decide *some* of the things we learn, I just think everyone would enjoy school more."

"May I tell you the value *I* see in students doing that?" Dr. Kittering asked.

Nutty almost fell out of his chair. "Sure," he said.

"If students help plan their own studies—what we call curriculum—they would have to think through the value of what they are learning. I can see that as very beneficial. If we had a committee and rotated the membership, eventually everyone could get a better picture of what education is all about."

"Uh . . . yeah. That's what I'm talking about. You just said it better."

Dr. Kittering laughed. This was going better than Nutty ever could have hoped.

"Frederick, I'm pleased that—"

"Most people call me Nutty."

"Maybe so. But I'm not going to."

"How about Freddie? That's what my parents call me."

"Okay. Freddie. I'm very impressed that you've given these matters some thought. I suspect you would make a good president. And I'm not going to take your name off the ballot. But I want the rest of this election raised to a higher plane."

"I know. I feel the same way. My friend says this is the way politics work—you know, all this negative stuff. But I don't think so. We don't have to start acting like a bunch of garbage mouths—just because the candidates for president and governor and everything act that way."

Dr. Kittering laughed again. "Yes, I certainly wouldn't want you to start acting like *adults*."

Now Nutty laughed. "My slogan is, 'I messed up last year, but this year I'll do a better job.' Maybe people who run for president of the United States could try that one."

Dr. Kittering seemed to like the idea.

Nutty went back to class, and he felt much better. Finally someone had taken his ideas seriously. Now, somehow, he just needed to get the kids to understand.

chapter 6

By the time Nutty sat down at his desk, he had an idea. What he needed to do was talk to all the kids, really level with them, and then tell them about his plans. Maybe the kids would be impressed if Nutty was honest with them, and if he told them what he wanted to do for the school. Who wouldn't want school to be more exciting?

So at noon, Nutty told his friends to spread the word. Right after school, on the front lawn, Nutty would give a "major address." He would answer all the charges against him.

And it worked. When school got out, a crowd gathered. Some had to catch buses, though, and Nutty knew he didn't have much time. He had to begin while he had an audience.

He stood on top of a retaining wall, near the front sidewalk, and Orlando introduced him: "You've been hearing a bunch of bad stuff about Nutty. But he's going to explain all that and tell you his plans. So listen to him." And then he shouted, "Hey, you guys. *Hey!* Shut up and listen."

"Thanks for that nice introduction," Nutty said, but no one laughed. Maybe he sounded too nervous. "Okay, here's what I want to tell you."

Kids did quiet down some.

"First, I want you to know that I wasn't a very good president last year. The things in that flier were mostly true."

Mindy and her friends came out of the building at about that time. Carrie yelled, "You heard it from an expert!"

A lot of kids laughed.

"I just want to tell the truth," Nutty said. "I—"

"The truth is, you don't know what you're doing!" some guy yelled.

"No. The truth is, I learned from my experience. I know what I can do now. I have some great plans."

"To do what? Peek in girls' windows?" a girl shouted.

"Hey, just a minute. I want to explain about that. I wasn't really peeking. I was just . . ."

"Staring."

"No. I—"

A bus pulled up, making a lot of noise. One group of kids started piling on. Nutty had to yell to be heard.

"I was only trying to catch Mindy writing one of those fliers. And I did. She was working on one—and her friends were helping her. I saw them."

"He's *lying!*" Mindy screamed. "We were doing posters."

Nutty was a little shaken by that. Either Mindy was the

greatest liar in the world, or she was telling the truth. She sounded very convincing.

"You're just a window peeker!" she shouted. "And now you're trying to make me look bad. Well, I'm not the one climbing around looking into people's *bedrooms*."

This got a big laugh and then a lot of catcalls.

"Watch out, girls. He might be looking in your window tonight!" April called out.

Nutty knew he was in deep trouble. He had to get off this subject.

"Listen," he said, "the main thing I wanted to tell you was that I have some plans for the school. Just think if we had more say about the things we learn. Wouldn't that make school more exciting?"

But most kids were paying no attention. They were heading for their buses or just wandering away.

Orlando said, "Never mind, Nutty. They aren't listening."

But Nutty was desperate now. "Are you going to vote for a girl who keeps writing rotten stuff about people?" he yelled.

"I didn't. You're a *liar!*" Mindy shouted back at him.

Nutty turned and faced her. "You're the liar!"

And then a kid who was just stepping on to his bus looked back and yelled, "They're both a couple of jerks. I'm voting for Denton!"

That idea seemed to create more enthusiasm than anything anyone had said the whole time.

"Give it up," Orlando muttered.

And Nutty did.

Nutty's friends told him it was time to drop out of the election. And Nutty knew they were probably right. But he wasn't ready to do that yet. The whole thing was no longer about winning; it was about having his say. And clearing his name. He at least wanted to speak at the campaign assembly and explain his side of the story—in a situation where kids would be forced to listen.

"If you're going to stay in, we better talk to William again," Richie said.

Nutty wasn't so sure that was a good idea, but he agreed to walk to William's house. When the boys got there, they had to wait for William to get home from his school. But when William finally arrived he seemed sort of amused—again—that the boys needed his help already.

The campaign staff gathered around William's kitchen table. William served up chocolate chip cookies and milk—with napkins—and he listened to what they all had to say.

By the time the story was out, he was shaking his head and looking deeply concerned. But Nutty could see a little hint of a smile at times, as though William thought of himself as above all this child's play.

William ate a cookie, very slowly, being careful not to drop crumbs on himself, and then he took a long drink of milk.

"Well, let's face it," he finally announced. "You're dead."

"Completely?" Richie asked.

"Dead is dead, Richie," William said. "Dead doesn't

come in degrees. People are not 'a little dead,' 'some dead,' or even 'mostly dead.' They're just *dead.*"

Nutty rather liked the image: He saw himself, white and clammy, stretched out on a slab of marble. Somehow that seemed better than standing up and facing people.

"So who's going to win?" Orlando asked.

"My guess is, Denton."

"And how long do you think kids will remember this whole window-peeking thing?"

"Oh, not for long. You might get some strange stares from adults in the community, however." For some reason, William thought that was rather funny.

"Maybe I should move," Nutty grumbled. "Maybe I can change my name and have plastic surgery done. Then the FBI can relocate me to some little town somewhere—where no one knows me."

"Yes, you might try the town of Peculiar, over by Kansas City. It's a nice little place, and something about the name makes me feel that you might fit right in."

Everybody was a comedian now.

William smiled. Nutty didn't.

But Richie said, "Maybe he's not finished off, yet. I've got an idea."

"If you're talking about the election, don't bother," Orlando said.

"But what about this? What if we wrote our own flier— and put in a bunch of stuff about Denton? That way, we could get some bad stuff going around about him too. Then we could plant the fliers in Mindy's desk. And everyone would say she's been lying about not writing those things."

"Richie, I'm surprised at you," William said. "That's a true dirty trick. You should work for a politician when you grow up."

"It's a *rotten* trick," Nutty said.

"True," William told him. "And it's not anything I approve of. But from a political point of view, it has its good points. You would only be showing Mindy up for what she really is, and at the same time, you could pin something negative on Denton."

"I thought you said Nutty was dead," Orlando said.

"Well, he probably is. But something of that sort might throw the whole election into confusion, give everyone a black eye, and maybe get Nutty back on even ground with the others."

"William, if something's rotten to do, it's rotten to do," Nutty said.

"That's a very moral position, Nutty. But think of it another way. Who is the best candidate? Who would actually serve the school best?"

"I don't know."

"No. Come on. Tell me what you think."

"I think I would."

William nodded, and he crossed his arms over his chest. "Then one way to look at this is that the most important thing you can do—to serve your school—is get yourself elected. You didn't start the dirty stuff, but if others want to play hardball, you have to play hardball too—or get knocked out of the batter's box."

It all sounded sort of reasonable. "Do you really think we should do something like that, William?" Nutty asked.

"Well, no. Of course not. But I'm merely saying that a politician might make that sort of argument."

Richie seemed to pay no attention to that. He was still thinking. "Look at it this way, Nutty," he said. "Right now, most of the kids in the school think you're a goof-up and a window peeker. You're trying to play it honest, and you're getting chewed up. That's not fair, is it?"

Nutty shrugged. Richie had a point. And if something would save his reputation, he . . . but no. "Look, I don't even *know* anything bad about Denton."

"Yeah, that's a problem," Orlando said. "He's sort of a nerd, but he's not a bad guy."

"Well, Nutty," William said, "I admire you. I think accepting this blow to your reputation and refusing to fight back is one of the more noble things I've seen in a person of your— or I mean, of *our*—age." William paused, cleared his throat, and then added, "But let me offer a little variation on Richie's concept. Just something to think about."

"I don't want to hear it," Nutty said.

"I do," Bilbo said.

"Well, fine. Nutty, just shut your ears, and I'll tell the other fellows."

"Yeah, right." But Nutty put his head down on the table, his forehead on his arms. He really didn't want to listen to all this.

59

"Think of it this way, fellows," William said. "As we listen to Nutty take this noble stand, we admire him. And we say to ourselves, 'What if everyone knew him as we do?' Surely, then, they would vote for him. True, we have seen him be a little less than consistent in his life—and sometimes less than responsible—maybe occasionally even rather scatterbrained. But still—"

"You can stop now, William," Nutty said. "I think *you* might be the one writing the fliers."

"Oh, no. I write more effectively—and I know more. I could really rip you up."

Nutty stood up. He was going to leave.

"Wait just a minute," William said. He cupped his hand around his chin and looked wise. "The point is, I really do consider you the best candidate. And you really are being remarkably honest. What I wish is that the entire student body would know the *real* you."

"So how do we do that?" Richie asked.

"Well, supposing you fellows staged something—something that might illustrate the real personality of our hero."

"Like what?" Orlando asked.

"Well . . . something like this. You do write up a flier about Denton. It wouldn't have to say much—or be that serious—because no one would actually read it."

"Why not?" Nutty said.

"You write the document and you plant it in Mindy's desk. But before Mindy finds it there, you challenge her in front of everyone. You claim she has now produced negative fliers against Denton and they are in her desk. She opens her desk to prove you wrong and—ta da!—there they are. You grab them, denounce her for her tactics, and you tear up the sheets. You could, of course, let one get out just to—"

"No."

"Well, fine. You tear them up, burn them, or whatever, and now the word gets out that Mindy has struck again. You show her up for what she is, and you show how honorable you are. You're suddenly a hero."

"That at least gets kids thinking that there *are* some bad things to say about Denton," Bilbo said.

"Exactly. And if you wanted to drop a few hints, you could mention—"

"No!" Nutty said again.

But he hadn't said no to the overall plan. He sort of liked the idea of the hero thing. All the same, he said, "William, it's still fake."

"Well, let me ask you this. If you knew Mindy was about to hand out negative fliers about Denton, and you knew they were in her desk, what would you do?"

"I don't know."

"Would you want the negative stuff to get out—and hurt Denton?"

"No. I already told you I don't like that."

"Wouldn't you want people to know what Mindy was up to—so they would finally know the truth about her?"

"Yeah."

"Well, then, what you would be doing—even though

staged—would give everyone the right impression of you. And I might add, of Mindy."

Nutty was thinking. William really was making sense. And what if by tomorrow everyone in the school were talking about his heroism—instead of his sleazy window peeking?

"Let me add one more element," William said. He waited and looked around. "Just suppose my editor friend at the local newspaper got wind of all this. And suppose he wrote up a story about the election at the lab school. And suppose the lead of the story was—with a little guidance from me—'Politics the way they ought to be.' Or something of that sort."

"You mean *fake*?" Orlando asked.

"Well, it all depends on how you look at it. But it would make a nice article. It has to be better than going back to school and hearing every day that you're *scum*."

Nutty was beginning to waver. He really was the sort of guy who would do something like that. And Mindy did have it coming.

"Okay, okay," Nutty said. "I'll do it. But we don't let anything get out about Denton."

"Wait a minute," William said. "I wasn't proposing that you actually do it. I was merely speculating about—"

"How are we going to get the sheets in her desk?" Richie asked. "Mr. Twitchell is always the first one there in the morning."

"There's that broken lock on the boys' bathroom window. Someone could get in at night," Bilbo said.

"How would we get into Twitchell's room?"

"The teachers leave the rooms open so Mr. Skinner can clean at night. That's no problem."

"We could get in *big-time* trouble if we got caught in the school," Nutty said.

"Yeah. We better not try that," Orlando said. "That's taking too big a chance."

"What do you think, William?" Nutty asked.

"Definitely too risky," William said. "I advise you not to do it."

But Nutty had come full circle now. He wanted to pull it off somehow. "I won't get anyone else in trouble," he said. "I'll write up the sheets, and I'll sneak in by myself."

All was silent for a time, but then Orlando said, "Well, if you're going to do it, I'll help you."

"Are you sure?"

"Yeah."

"You know what happened in the tree."

"I know. But going into the school at night—all by yourself—that's pretty scary. You need someone to go with you."

"Should we do it tonight?"

"Yeah. We can write the fliers on my computer. My printer looks about the same as hers. And I think my dad has some paper that's sort of the same."

"Okay."

But William stood up. "Fellows, I don't know. This was all just theory. I don't know that it's a very good idea. The breaking-in part especially concerns me."

"If we pull it off, will you still talk to the guy at the newspaper?" Nutty asked.

"Well, yes. I suppose I can do that."

"All right, then. We go tonight."

chapter 7

By the time Nutty got home he was already second-guessing the new plan. He told himself that he was backing out. The whole thing was wrong. And wrong was wrong. He would simply take his name off the ballot and forget the whole thing.

But every time he got that far, he realized that one of the steps down that road was to tell his parents that he was withdrawing from the election.

That was not going to be easy.

Still, he had to do it.

Nutty tried to get the timing right. Dad came rushing into the house a little late and said he had an appointment in forty minutes. Mom said, "If you'll throw a salad together, I'll—"

"That's all right. Let's go grab a sandwich," Dad said. He was trying to become a modern husband, but the truth was, he didn't like to do much of anything in the kitchen.

"Fred, I just don't like all the fat content in the food at those fast-food places," Mom told him. So Dad was soon tearing up a head of lettuce and slicing red cabbage. Mom was boiling some sort of pasta.

"We never eat any meat around this place anymore," Dad mumbled to Nutty—but he didn't dare say it to his wife.

Nutty figured the mood wasn't just right to break the news.

He held on until Dad was saying, "That marinara sauce is excellent, honey," and Mom was telling him what a nice job he had done on the salad.

"I decided not to run for president after all," Nutty said, and he tried to sound casual.

"What? I thought you already signed up," Dad said.

"I did. But—you know—I don't need to be president two years in a row."

That seemed to go down all right. Dad looked a little disappointed, but Mom said, "Well, that's true." And Nutty thought he was home free.

He gave Suzie a hard stare that said, Don't say a word, you little creep.

Suzie got the message.

And rejected it.

"He has to drop out. He has no chance to win after all the stupid things he's done."

"What stupid things?" Dad asked, and he looked concerned.

"He almost got caught—"

"Suzie, be quiet. That's not even true."

But Suzie kept right on going. "—by the police. He climbed a tree and tried to peek in Mindy's window."

"Freddie!" Mom said. *"What?"*

Suzie smiled and cocked her nose in the air, flipped her curly hair back, and said, with her eyes, I got you, Nutty.

"It wasn't what you think, Mom," Nutty was saying. Then he told his version of what had happened.

"That's terrible," Dad said. "Why would Mindy hand out such awful stuff?"

Nutty shrugged.

"So now everyone in the school thinks you're a window peeker?" Mom asked, and she looked almost sick.

"They know he is," Suzie said, with joy. "He admitted it."

Nutty reached under the table and grabbed Suzie by the knee. He squeezed hard, but she only jumped and slammed her other knee against the table, making all the plates bounce.

Mom and Dad both jumped in response, and then Suzie said, "He grabs girls' legs under the table too."

"That's enough, Freddie," Dad said. Nutty could see that Dad's concern was turning to panic. "Son," he said, "you can't withdraw. That would leave you in disgrace. You have to fight—and win. You have to make sure kids know the truth about you."

"I doubt I can win now, Dad."

"He never could win," Suzie said.

"Suzie, that's enough," Dad said. And he gave the issue

some thought. "Freddie, I have to sell insurance in this town. I need to keep *my* reputation. I can't have everyone thinking that my kids are a mess."

"I'm not a mess," Suzie said. "I never get in any trouble."

"I can stay in the election if you want," Nutty said to his dad, ignoring his little sister. "But I don't know what good it will do."

"You better think of *some* way to clear your name. That's what you better do."

Nutty nodded, and then he let his breath blow out. He was back to where he had started: the plan.

So Nutty rinsed off his dish and put it in the dishwasher, and then he walked to Orlando's.

Orlando had come up with just the right paper. He let Nutty do the typing on the computer, but they thought together what to say—which wasn't much.

Orlando thought he knew the right font to make the type look the same as the one Mindy had been using. He tried it, and they printed out a trial copy.

"That's good," Nutty said. "That looks about the same." He looked over the text again. "We'll just give kids a quick glance at it anyway."

The boys printed off a few copies. They figured they didn't need a ton. But already, Nutty was feeling uneasy again. "Do you think we ought to sneak into the school?" he asked Orlando.

"Not really," Orlando said, which was not what Nutty

expected. "I still think it might be best if you just drop out and then let this whole thing blow over for a while."

"I'm staying in, Orlando."

"Then I guess we have to sneak into the school."

"We better wait until it gets dark."

So the boys waited. They watched a little TV and they waited for the sun to set. Nutty kept getting more nervous all the time.

By the time they had moved in behind the bushes at the front of the school, Nutty could hear his heart beating in his ears. But Orlando pushed on the boys' bathroom window, and it opened—just as they had known it would.

Nutty gave Orlando a foothold with his hands, and Orlando pulled himself up enough to get his head and shoulders in the window. "Give me a little push," he whispered.

Nutty, in his nervousness, pushed a little too hard. Orlando suddenly disappeared through the window and went crashing to the floor.

"Are you okay?" Nutty called after him.

"No, you idiot," Orlando mumbled from deep within the boys' bathroom. Nutty figured he must still be on the floor.

"What did you hurt?"

"Everything!"

"Orlando, really, are you all right?"

But now his face appeared in the window. "I said, 'Give me a little push,' not, 'Shove as hard as you can.'"

"Sorry about that."

"Tell that to my shoulder and my arm and my hip and about ten other places that are bruised."

"Just be quiet. I'm coming in."

Nutty reached up and got hold of the windowsill, and he clambered up the side of the building, using the grip of his sneakers to help. He got his head in the window, and worked his body through, and then he whispered, "Help me, so I won't fall."

"Why should I?"

"Come on, Orlando."

So Orlando grabbed him and pulled him through. But Nutty's weight was a little much for Orlando. The two crashed to the floor, with Nutty on top.

"Oh, man," Orlando moaned. "Now you finished me off. I'm going to die in the school bathroom. That's sick."

Nutty rolled off and whispered, "Orlando, quit making so much noise."

Orlando didn't like that. "You *jumped* on me, Nutty. And then you blame *me* for making noise?"

But Nutty was feeling his way through the dark boys' room, his hands touching the doors to the stalls. "Now be quiet. I'm going to open the door. We need to make sure no one's in the building."

"Don't worry. No one's here."

"Just let me check."

Nutty slowly opened the door. He looked into the darkness. No light anywhere. "Okay, let's go," he whispered.

He stepped slowly, quietly into the hallway, and then felt Orlando crash into his back.

"What are you doing?" Nutty said, way too loudly.

"Well, what are you walking so slow for?"

"Because I can't see anything."

"Just put your hand on the wall."

"I will, if you'll get out of the way."

"Nutty, don't be so—"

But they both heard the noise at the same time. It was the sound of a door shutting, a long way off. Nutty froze. He tried to think what to do.

He reached for the wall and put his hand on something warm and soft and—ugly.

"Get your hand out of my face."

"We gotta get out of here," Nutty said.

"No. We're okay. Mr. Skinner must be cleaning rooms. He's around the corner and way down in the other hallway. He'll probably go from one room to the next. Let's just hurry to Twitchell's room and then we can go out the back door."

"Okay. Let's go."

The two started moving down the hallway, touching the wall, feeling the lockers and the doors. But Nutty moved slowly, and Orlando kept stepping on his heels.

When they reached the door, Nutty tried the knob and found the door unlocked. But he pulled the door open—right into Orlando's face.

"Be careful," Orlando moaned. "Now my nose is broken."

"Quit your crying. I didn't hit you that hard."

Nutty suddenly took a shot in the back. But he let it go. He stepped into the room. "Don't turn the light on," he said. "We'll just count the desks."

And then he remembered. "Oh, no!"

"What?"

"I left the fliers outside."

"What?"

"I set them on the ground when I was helping you get in the window."

"Nutty, let's just get out of here and forget this whole thing. I don't think you were *meant* to be president."

"No. I'll go out the back door, run around to the front, and get the fliers. You wait at the door and let me back in."

"No way."

"I'll run fast."

"Yeah, while I stay here and get caught."

"Just stay by the back doors. If Skinner comes down the hallway, you can step out and be gone."

"Oh, man."

But that meant he agreed.

So Orlando and Nutty found their way back to the classroom door, and then hurried to the end of the hallway and around a little bend to the back door. Nutty pushed his way out the doors and then dashed around the building. At least he found the fliers quickly. They hadn't blown away, as he feared they might have.

He made the long run back, and when he tapped on the door, Orlando let him back in.

Everything was all right now. They got back to Twitchell's classroom, stumbled to the front of the room, found the second row, third seat, and planted the fliers.

"Okay. We're set. Now let's get out of here."

They headed for the door and were about to open it when the hall light came on.

Orlando crashed into Nutty's back before he saw what Nutty had seen—the light coming under the door.

"Oh, *no!*" he said.

"He's going to be doing the rooms down this way now," Nutty said. "What if he starts at this end?"

"Window!" Orlando said.

They both hurried to the windows. But the windows didn't open very far—just enough to let a little air in.

"We're dead," Orlando said. "Why do I let you get me into these things?"

"Shut up. We'll get out of here. We've got to see what he's doing."

So the boys went back to the door, and Nutty cracked it ever so slightly.

And then pulled it shut again!

"He's sweeping the hallway floor, heading this way."

Orlando clapped himself against the wall. "I'm too young to die," he whined.

In a moment, they heard the footsteps, the gentle rubbing

of the soft broom. The sound passed and then a few seconds later, came back the other way.

Once the sound was well away, Nutty said, "He'll do the hall, and then he'll start on the rooms. If he starts at the other end, we're okay."

"And if he starts at this end, he's got us."

"Well . . . yeah." Nutty had to think. "Okay. Here's what we'll do. He's making long passes up and down the hallway. We'll wait until he goes by this time and starts back up the hall. Then we'll make a run for it. We're only about ten steps from the corner."

"He'll hear us."

"We'll tiptoe."

"Too slow."

"Okay. We'll run, turn the corner, hit the doors, and be outside. He may hear us, but by the time he turns around, we'll be gone. Once outside, we head for the hiding place—in case he tries to chase us."

But now the sound was coming back.

It passed, and then passed again. Nutty whispered. "Wait. Wait." And then, "Okay, let's go."

He opened the door slowly, spotted Skinner, still moving away, and then opened the door the rest of the way.

As Orlando crashed into him.

Suddenly the two were running hard. They rounded the corner, hit the door, jumped through, and ran hard around the building.

On the side of the building was a favorite hiding place,

under some bushes. Nutty and Orlando dove in, then curled up against the side of the building. And listened. But they heard nothing. Skinner hadn't followed. They seemed to be safe.

"Do you think he heard us?" Nutty asked.

"I know he *heard* us. The only question is, did he *see* us?"

chapter 8

Orlando and Nutty decided to split up and each head to his own house—just in case Skinner had called the police. So Nutty cut across the university campus toward his home.

But Nutty saw no patrol cars, heard no sirens, and he figured he was okay. Skinner had surely heard them, but he must not have been too concerned. He and Orlando had pulled it off.

Then why did Nutty feel so strange?

He tried not to think about it. He would just go home and sit tight, and in the morning he would do what he had to do.

But he still felt . . . sort of . . . not just strange. Sort of . . . crummy.

The plan was okay, he told himself. He tried to remember all the stuff William had said. Nutty was only showing himself for what he really was—by faking something that he really would do if the opportunity had actually come up. That was honest—basically. It was just a roundabout *kind* of honesty.

That wasn't so bad, was it?

But Nutty suddenly felt the need to talk to someone— sort things out a little. He had always talked to William at times like this, and he was tempted to do that now. But he knew what William would say.

He thought of Sarah.

Nutty had never actually gone to Sarah's house by himself. He had never even spent much time with her alone. He wasn't sure he dared do that now. But her house was in the same direction as his own, and when he got to his place, he noticed that his feet kept taking him right on down the street toward Sarah's.

Strange, what feet chose to do sometimes.

But it was his finger that really surprised him. After his feet got him onto Sarah's front porch, he never in the world expected his finger to press the doorbell. But it did. And suddenly he panicked. His mouth would soon have to take over this whole operation.

But his feet were being stubborn now that they had come this far. "Hi, is Sarah home?"

The worst. It was Sarah's little brother. And of course, he had to yell, "Hey, Sarah, Nutty's here to see you!" He said it with a singsong, teasing tone. That was bad enough, but then he added, "At least he came to the door instead of peeking in your window."

Nutty's finger suddenly had an impulse to get into the action again. It wanted to poke the kid in the eye.

But then Sarah appeared. "Hi," she said, and she was clearly surprised.

"Hi." And then Nutty just stood there waiting for his mouth to do something. Maybe seven or eight seconds went by.

Seven seconds can be a very long time when two people are staring at each other—and one is trying to think what in the world to say. But Nutty's throat had closed off and was unwilling to clear itself, even after three good "ahems."

"Did you want to come in or something?" Sarah finally said.

"Uh, no."

Four more seconds, maybe, but they seemed longer than the first seven.

"Did you—"

"Do you want to come out and . . . talk?"

Only two seconds this time. But they were two terrible, miserable, humiliating seconds.

"I guess so." She stepped onto the porch and shut the door behind her. But she waited, as though she expected Nutty to have something to say.

Nutty had never thought that far ahead. But he wasn't going to allow any more seconds to pass, so he said, "It's a nice night."

Sarah gave him an odd look. "It's *humid*," she said.

This was not a good sign. She didn't sound at all friendly.

"Yeah, it's not that great of a night—actually."

She was still staring at him.

"I just . . . wanted to talk."

"What about?"

"Uh . . . I don't know. Maybe the campaign."

"Nutty, we didn't write those fliers. You have no right to keep telling people that."

"Are you sure?"

"What do you mean?"

"Well, we saw you."

"Oh, really? From the tree?" She didn't say, "you low-life, window-peeking scum," but Nutty could tell that's what she meant.

"Yeah. I'm sorry about doing that. But we did see you. And you weren't doing posters. Mindy was sitting at her computer, and you girls were all telling her what to write."

"Nutty, Mindy doesn't even have a computer in her room. The only computer the Marshalls have is downstairs in a little office room."

Now Nutty was staring at Sarah. This was terrible. "Were you guys all crowded around . . . something?"

"No. We were spread out around the room—on the floor."

"You *never* crowded around a desk or something like that? Not once, the whole time you were there?"

"No. Not ever. Mindy doesn't have a desk."

"But Orlando said you were all—"

"You didn't see us yourself?"

"Well . . . no."

"You mean everyone is saying you're a window peeker and it was really Orlando?"

"We were both in the tree. Orlando was just a little higher. But don't tell anyone."

"Fine. I won't. But I will tell you this much. For some reason, Orlando is lying to you."

Sarah was still standing with her back to the door, as though she were planning to turn and go back in the house at any time. Nutty was standing in front of her, straight and stiff, like a soldier being inspected.

Something was wrong, way wrong, and Nutty couldn't think how to explain it. But she was right. Someone was lying to him—and it had to be Sarah, or it had to be Orlando. He didn't want to believe either possibility.

"Well, anyway," Nutty said, "I really did *think* you girls were doing it. Who else would? I don't think Denton would."

"I don't know, Nutty."

Nutty was standing there, and seconds had started to tick away again. "Could I ask you about something else?" he finally said.

She nodded, but she didn't move from the door.

"Could we sit down or something?" He had spotted an old wicker love seat on the front porch—although he called it a "chair" in his own mind.

Sarah did walk over and sit down, and he thought he saw

her relax just a little. Nutty sat down next to her. "Do you think I should drop out of the election?" he asked.

"That's up to you, Nutty. But I don't think you can win now."

"Do you think Mindy will?"

"Probably." She was sitting absolutely as far away from him as she could get, and she was leaning over the edge of the . . . chair. Cicadas were screeching in unison, and the air was thick and heavy. Nutty was no longer sure his feet had been right in bringing him here.

"Why do you even want to be president again?" Sarah finally asked.

"Well, I have some ideas—some stuff I want to do."

"You aren't really serious about that, are you?"

"Yeah, I'm serious."

"I thought it was something William told you to say."

"William used to tell me what to say. But he doesn't anymore. These are my own ideas."

"Like what?"

"I just think that kids would learn better if they were in on planning what we study. I talked to Dr. Kittering about it, and she thought it was a good idea."

"Nutty, is this for real?"

"*Yeah.* Don't you think I ever . . . think?"

She laughed. "I never noticed you doing a whole lot of it before."

Nutty smiled. "Well, I never think so much that it gets in the way of all the other stuff I like to do."

She laughed even more, and she suddenly sounded rather friendly. "So what is this? Are you starting to get . . . *mature* . . . or something like that?"

"That's me. Nutty, the *ma-tuuurrre* guy."

"When you got us out of the movie last summer—that was kind of mature. But I thought you just hated it so much that you wanted out. I didn't know you had started to *think* in your spare time."

She was teasing, but she actually seemed to be impressed with Nutty.

Nutty's thoughts, however, were still back on the movie. "Just think if Mr. Deveraux had released that stinky film. We both would have been . . . *humiliated.*"

"I know. The script was so stupid," she said. "Remember all those stupid things we had to say? You would look into my eyes and say, 'I love you deeply. I love you—'"

"'Elizabeth, you are part of me—no, you *are* me, and I am you.'" Nutty said the line with gooey exaggeration.

"Oh, yeah. That was it. You kept saying it and saying it. And old Deveraux kept screaming at you."

"What about that day we kissed about twenty times, and he wouldn't let us stop?"

"Twenty-*three*! And it was hot and sticky, and he just kept making you say those dumb lines and then kiss me over and over and over. It was the most sickening thing I ever did in my whole life."

Nutty agreed—mostly—but he wasn't exactly in love

with the way she said it. He managed to smile a little and say, "Yeah, that was bad."

But she seemed to sense that she had said the wrong thing. Nutty saw her come within an inch of apologizing, but then she let it go. They both just looked at each other. Nutty thought of saying, "Right now, though, it wouldn't be so bad," but he pushed the thought away, quickly.

And the two looked away from each other.

Nutty didn't hear the cicadas now, didn't think about the warm night, didn't even think what he was going to say next. What he did notice was that Sarah had shifted in the seat, ever so slightly. She didn't move toward him, but she wasn't leaning over the end of the armrest anymore. She was maybe straight up, or maybe—just possibly—leaning slightly toward him.

It was time to go.

"Nutty, I do think you'd be a better president than Mindy or Denton. You weren't last year, but I think you would be this year."

"Thanks," Nutty said. And he was taken by surprise.

Somewhere, birds had begun to sing. Nutty was sure of it.

"I'm proud of you that you're actually thinking about stuff that would make the school better."

Or was it an orchestra? Nutty thought he heard violins.

And then she touched his arm.

"Good luck," she said—softly.

Nutty got up. He floated off the porch; he winged like an eagle down the street, the air current carrying him home. And all the way he felt the touch, still lingering on his arm. And he heard those words, full of meaning and power and *warmth*. "Good luck," she had said.

It was so beautiful.

He said it out loud to himself. And he tried to imitate that soft, sweet voice.

How could she say something like that? What if her parents had heard her? What if her little brother had been listening in? Wouldn't they have known what Nutty now knew? The words were "Good luck," but the *meaning* . . . well, that was *obvious*.

Nutty wandered into the house, bumping into the door frame on the way. Then he bumped gently off the walls as he floated to his room. There, he lay on his bed. But he soon floated to the ceiling. And there he stayed until a crushing thought slammed him back on his own bed.

What had he gone there to talk to her about—really?

What would she think of him if she knew the *act* he was going to put on the next morning?

The whole thing suddenly felt dishonest, disgusting, *rotten*.

Sarah would hate him if she knew what he had planned.

chapter 9

Nutty knew what he had to do. He had to go back to the school and pull those fliers out of Mindy's desk. And then he had to call all his friends and tell them that the whole thing was off.

He would go before the school at the campaign assembly and come clean. He would admit his past mistakes and then present his ideas. If the students liked them, fine, and if not, so be it. But he wouldn't try to pull off this staged hero act, whether it would help him or not.

Nutty hurried down to the front door and slipped out—before his parents knew he had ever been home. School was only a ten-minute walk, but this time Nutty ran all the way. By the time he got to the boys' room window, he was breathing hard, but he pushed it open, and he leaped to get a good grip. Then he pulled himself up and in.

He landed on the boys' room floor, more or less the way

Orlando had, but he didn't take time to feel sorry for himself. He jumped up and hurried to the door. He peeked out and saw no light, heard nothing but his own heavy breathing. Skinner was finished and had left.

This time he hurried down the hallway. He entered the room and felt his way along the desks until he found the right one. Then he opened the desk and grabbed the fliers.

Mission accomplished.

He felt better already.

He worked his way back along the desks, found the door, opened it, and stepped into the hallway. He was about to turn and walk to the door, finally not feeling the need to run—when he heard footsteps.

He froze. And the footsteps stopped.

Maybe they had never been there.

But he heard breathing. Was it still his own?

No.

For at least ten seconds he waited, hearing the breathing, sensing that someone was there, not all that far away. If it was Skinner, what was he doing there? Who else could it be?

Suddenly Nutty took off. He darted for the door, and now he heard the footsteps again.

He grabbed the door, opened it, but then stopped and listened. He could hear someone running, not chasing him but heading back up the hallway. Maybe it was Skinner. Maybe he was running for the light—or to call the police.

Nutty blasted out the door and spun around the corner.

He charged to the hiding place, behind the bushes, and he dove in. And he waited. But he heard nothing, and he didn't know what to do next.

Maybe he should make a dash across campus and head for home. But Skinner might call campus security. Maybe he should dodge around to the front of the school and then take a long way back to his house. But what if the town police were on the way?

Somehow there was comfort in this hiding place for the moment. He wanted to wait and see whether he heard anything before he ventured out.

And then he heard someone running. Now he knew he was in trouble. People must be looking for him. He held still, and didn't breathe as the steps came closer.

And closer.

And then someone dove into the bushes and right on top of him.

Nutty let out a scream of surprise and so did the guy who had just captured him. But the guy rolled off and gasped, "What are you doing here?"

"What?"

By now, Nutty knew, but he still couldn't believe it. It was Orlando.

"What's going on?" Orlando grunted.

Suddenly one part of all this was making sense. "Were you inside the school just now?" Nutty asked.

"Yeah. Was that you?"

"Yeah. I thought you were Skinner."

"I thought *you* were."

Nutty was laughing now, but he still wondered why in the world Orlando would come back to the school.

"What were you doing?" Orlando asked.

"I came back to pull those fliers out of the desk. I didn't want to go through with it." Nutty couldn't see Orlando, but he sensed a sudden awkwardness in the silence that followed. "What were *you* doing in there?"

"Same thing," Orlando said, but he sounded tense.

"Why?"

"I just . . . decided it wasn't a good idea. You know—not fair, and stuff like that."

Nutty didn't believe that, mostly because Orlando sounded stiff and nervous. He was lying.

"Hey, that's *my* decision. Why didn't you call me or something?"

"I don't know." Orlando hesitated. "I guess I figured I was in on it too. But—you know—I didn't feel right about it. I was going to call you and tell you I couldn't go through with it—after I got the fliers."

That sounded fairly believable—the words. But Orlando was lying and Nutty knew it. And he now knew it wasn't the first time.

Orlando moved and Nutty heard something rustle—paper.

"What are you doing?"

"Nothing." The rustling stopped.

Nutty reached for Orlando and touched his shoulder. He

could tell that Orlando had shifted, that he was reaching under the bushes.

Nutty suddenly reached across Orlando and grabbed his arm. Then he squirmed over the top of him and grasped his hand.

Empty.

But just beyond Orlando's hand, Nutty felt papers on the ground. He got hold of them and rolled off Orlando. Then he scooted out from under the bushes.

"What is this, Orlando?" It was too dark to see what was on the papers. But Nutty was pretty sure he knew.

"Nothing. Give me those."

Nutty started to walk toward one of the overhead lights that illuminated a nearby campus sidewalk, but Orlando grabbed at his arm and tried to take the sheets back. Nutty pulled loose and ran for the light.

He got there a second ahead of Orlando and caught a quick glance. The papers were fliers, like the others that had been appearing all week.

Orlando grabbed again. "Nutty, give me those!" he shouted, and he sounded desperate. But Nutty squirmed and held the papers out under the light long enough to read the headline: Nutty Nutsell Plants Phony Fliers.

And then Nutty knew.

"You've been doing these all along, haven't you?" he said. His voice was little more than a whisper. He was more shocked than angry.

Orlando quit struggling and stepped away, out of the light.

"Why?"

Orlando still didn't answer. Nutty looked down and read more of the flier. It told the whole story about the planning session, the decision to pull off a fake noble act, and the plan to get the story in the newspaper.

"What were you going to do with these—put them in Mindy's desk?"

"None of your business," Orlando said, and he turned and started walking away.

"Come on, Orlando. What's going on? Why would you do this?"

Orlando just kept walking. Nutty followed.

"You were going to make sure I didn't tear them up, weren't you? You were going to let these get out."

"Yup."

"Hey, I would have known you did it. How did you think you were going to get away with it?"

"I didn't care that much, if you want to know the truth. I was going to tell you we had a leak in our organization—the same as I told you before. If you bought it, fine. If not, that was all right too."

Nutty suddenly hurried, got in front of Orlando, and turned around. He grabbed him by the shoulders and stopped him. "Orlando, I thought we were best friends."

"Well, I guess that's over now."

Nutty dropped his hands. The wind could have blown him right out of town. He was suddenly empty, even light-headed. "Do you hate me or something?" he asked.

Orlando took a long breath. Finally he said, "No. But I'm tired of you getting everything you want. You were president *last year*. You didn't have to be president again."

"Why should that bother you?"

Orlando didn't answer.

But Nutty suddenly realized. "Did you want to run?"

"Maybe."

"Why didn't you say something?"

"I started to—that day in the hall. And then you just walked in the office and got your petition."

"If you had said something, I would have let you run—and then I would have helped you."

"Yeah, right."

"Really, Orlando. I would have."

But Orlando wasn't convinced. He moved around Nutty and began walking down the street again. Nutty caught up and walked alongside him. He was starting to remember all the stuff that had come out in those fliers. "Orlando, that was *awful* stuff you wrote about me."

"It was all true. You said so yourself."

"It was still rotten to write it." Orlando didn't answer. But the reality of what Orlando had done was finally settling into Nutty's mind, and the anger was growing in him. "And it was rotten to make everyone think Mindy did it."

"Hey, I guess I'm just a rotten guy. You can write your own flier now—and tell everyone what I did."

"That's just what I'm going to do too."

"Be my guest."

"Orlando, you've been doing everything you can to ruin me, and the whole time you've been acting like you're my big buddy. That's *scummy*. And I still haven't heard you say you're sorry."

"I'm *not* sorry," Orlando said, and he picked up his pace.

Nutty stopped and let him go. "I'm never going to speak to you again as long as I live, Orlando."

Orlando just kept going.

Nutty felt as though someone had clubbed him over the head. He walked home and then went straight to his room. He needed to think.

He sat on his bed for a long time, and he kept picturing Orlando at all those meetings, lying, putting the blame on Mindy. He had lied about what he had seen in Mindy's room, and then he had gone home and reported Nutty for being a window peeker in the next flier. Except, of course, he had left out the little detail about his being in the tree *with* Nutty.

And Nutty had been keeping that a secret—to protect his buddy.

This was unbelievable.

Nutty didn't think anyone, ever, could be that . . . rotten. Rotten, rotten, rotten. The word just kept pounding though his head.

He finally walked out to the kitchen and called William. Keeping his voice down, he told the story—at least a very short version of it.

William said he wasn't surprised. He had had some suspicions of that sort. Then he said, "Nutty, I know you're disappointed, but I'm not sure why you're so surprised."

"What?"

"Jealousy, Nutty. Jealousy. You were president. You were the star of the basketball team. You got the part in the movie. Orlando always has to stand around and watch you get all the attention."

"That's no excuse for doing something that . . . *rotten*."

"No. Of course not. I'm just saying it's not all that surprising."

"I'm going to tell everyone what he did."

"I can understand why you would want to do that."

"You mean you don't think I *should*?"

"Nutty, I promised you that I wouldn't try to tell you what to do anymore. I'm certainly not going to give you any advice on this issue."

"But you think it's wrong to tell on him, don't you?"

"I didn't say that. A person could make the argument that he needs to be brought to justice and properly punished for such behavior."

"That's *exactly* what I think—no matter what you think. Good-bye."

Nutty hung up the phone and walked back to his room.

He sat on his bed and thought the whole thing through— several times. And now he knew what he would do. For a couple of days he would let Orlando stew. He wouldn't put out a flier; he wouldn't say a word. And he would stop campaigning for president.

But at the campaign assembly he would get up and withdraw his name from the ballot. Then he would say, "But I do want to set some things straight." And he would tell the whole story.

Above all, when it was over, all the kids would know that *Orlando* was the real window peeker, and a big *liar*. Nutty wouldn't be president, but at least he could clear his name.

Well, maybe not clear it. But at least he wouldn't look quite so bad.

He felt good about that.

But when he went to bed, he couldn't go to sleep. He kept thinking about Orlando, his best friend, being such a *backstabber*. It was too terrible—too *rotten*—to imagine.

He could hardly wait to get back at the guy.

chapter *10*

For the next few days Nutty kept a low profile. Mindy was turning up the heat on her campaign. She had posters all over the walls, and every day, before and after school, she had her supporters outside begging for votes.

Nutty didn't campaign, didn't really say much. When kids gave him a hard time, or started to tease him about the window-peeking thing, he just said, "I think you should vote for Denton. That's what I plan to do."

That word got back to Mindy pretty fast, and she really didn't know what to do. Sarah told Nutty that Mindy was still expecting some big trick, maybe some help from William. That's why she was still campaigning so hard.

Nutty told Sarah, "If everyone who doesn't like Mindy votes for Denton, he'll win by a landslide." But he didn't tell her that he was pulling his name off the ballot.

Denton put up a few posters, but he didn't really act as though he cared a whole lot.

Bilbo and Richie knew very quickly that Nutty and Orlando were not speaking to each other, but neither Nutty nor Orlando would say why. Nutty heard Orlando say to Richie, "Ask Nutty what's going on. I'm sure he can't wait to tell you."

But Nutty told Richie, "I'll tell you some other time. I don't feel like talking about it yet." He only told Richie and Bilbo not to bother about campaigning.

On the night before the campaign speech, however, Nutty called William one more time. He told him all the reasons he was going to tell the kids what Orlando had done.

William listened. "Well, I can understand that," William said. "I'm sure you would never double-cross a friend the way he did."

"What's that supposed to mean, William?" Nutty said. "I *wouldn't*. I never have."

"I know. That's what I said."

"Yeah. But now you're saying I'm double-crossing Orlando."

"No. I didn't say that."

"You don't have to. I know what you're thinking. But Orlando was *rotten*, and he's going to pay for it."

"I understand."

William could be infuriating. "Look, I've been honest in this campaign. You wanted me to do all kinds of phony tricks, but I wouldn't do *any* of them. And now, rather than do that stuff, I'm pulling out of the election."

"Excuse me, Nutty. But you fellows came to me and

asked what you could do to save your campaign. I suggested various ploys that politicians have been known to use, but I never tried to talk you into any of them. In fact, I admired your stand against them."

"William, you . . . oh, never mind. I'm not listening to you anymore. I'm making up my own mind about this."

"I thought you had already made up your mind."

"I have."

"Well, fine. I hope you feel good about it when it's all over."

"William, you have no right to say that to me." Nutty slammed the phone back on the hook. What did William think he was—Nutty's conscience or something?

Orlando was a traitor, and he deserved what he was going to get.

When Nutty went to bed that night, he went over his talk in his mind. He would thank his friends—his real friends—for supporting him, and then he would announce his withdrawal. After that, he would say, "Now that I'm no longer running for president, I want to tell you some things, just so everyone will know the whole truth. This has been a dirty campaign, but the wrong people have been blamed for it. I think everyone deserves to know the truth."

Something like that. Every time he went over it, he thought of different ways to say it, or he added little wrinkles. But it always built to the point where he said, "Orlando Ortega is the guy who wrote those negative fliers—while he pretended to be my friend. And he's the same guy who did everything he could to let others take the blame. I've never known anyone who did anything so *rotten* in my whole life."

Each time Nutty came to the end of his little speech, he told himself that he would go to sleep. But then the speech would start up again. And when he finally did drift off, the speech started happening in his dreams.

It was a long night, and a long day that followed. Nutty was glad when the time finally came for the assembly, and he could finally get this whole thing behind him.

As he sat on the little stage in the cafeteria and the students marched in with their chairs, he let the words run through his mind one last time. He had made up a note card, but the talk had sunk deeply into his mind, and he was sure he wouldn't need the card.

The candidates for secretary spoke first, and then the vice-presidential candidates. Most of the talks were short and very rehearsed—and kind of stupid. No one had any real reasons to run, other than that they wanted to win.

Sarah's talk was much better than the others, however. She told the students, "I believe a school only runs well when everyone works together—students and teachers and principal. I know that Dr. Kittering wants to hear our opinions about things, and I will do all I can to find out what you want, and to make sure those things are brought up in council meetings."

She got a lot of applause. And Nutty was proud of her. Maybe her friends were making most of the noise. Or maybe boys were clapping because she was so cute. Nutty wasn't sure the students had really paid any attention to the things she had said.

The presidential candidates spoke in alphabetical order, Denton first. His talk lasted approximately eighteen seconds. "If you vote for me, I'll try to do my best," was probably his hardest-hitting sentence. It was almost the only one.

Mindy got up next. Her talk lasted more like eighteen *hours*. Actually, it was probably only five minutes or so, but it was full of grand, flowery words that didn't really add up to anything. She never got around to saying one word about what she wanted to do as president. The main idea seemed to be: I'm really excited about this, and I want to win, so vote for me.

She did say, "Some people made up some lies about me and said that I wrote some negative stuff about one of the candidates. But I want you to know that I didn't do that. I don't know who wrote those fliers, but I didn't. Nutty . . . or I mean, the candidate . . . did say the stuff in the fliers was true, though, so I guess it wasn't such a mean thing to do, in a way. But I *didn't* do it, and none of my supporters did. Because I asked all of them, and they said they didn't. So don't let that candidate tell you different, or anything like that."

"Oh, brother," Nutty mumbled under his breath, but he told himself all that didn't matter anymore. He was mainly just looking forward to his chance to get up to the podium.

The sixth-graders were sitting in the back of the room.

Nutty spotted Orlando in the very back row. He looked miserable, the way he had ever since Nutty had caught him with the fliers.

Nutty had to admit, the guy had never made up a bunch of phony apologies and begged Nutty not to say anything. He had just waited. By now Orlando must have figured out that Nutty was holding his ammunition for this big moment when *everyone* would be there.

Nutty realized that Mindy was actually—finally—wrapping up her talk. "A vote for me is a vote for the future. I will make the lab school the best school *anywhere*. I will work with all my heart and soul to make you proud of me, proud of the lab school, and proud to be Americans."

Blah, blah, blah. Nutty slid toward the front of his chair.

Mindy walked back to her seat and Dr. Kittering announced, "And now our final presidential candidate, Frederick Nutsell."

The kids all laughed—maybe at "Frederick," but probably also because they knew what a mess Nutty was in.

He walked to the podium, and he took a breath. This wasn't at all the way he had imagined it. Kids were squirming around, talking, acting like they didn't care.

Nutty couldn't remember how his talk was supposed to start. "I . . . uh . . . don't want to be president," he finally said. "I'm not running anymore. I just want my name taken off the ballot."

The room was suddenly silent.

"But I want to tell you why."

Nutty took a long breath. He couldn't remember a single word of his talk.

"I know it was kind of weird to run for president a second time," he heard himself saying. "I know I wasn't a very good president last year, but I thought I could do better if I tried again."

This got a laugh—which Nutty hadn't expected.

"No, I mean it. I thought if I ran again, I could do some good stuff. Kids don't learn as much as they could because someone always just tells them what to learn. I told Dr. Kittering that I thought we students should have some say in what we learn. And she told me some people believe that kids will only really learn things they want to know. What I wanted to do was find out what kinds of stuff kids were curious to know about—and then have them do projects and reports and stuff. And I thought we could get some of the professors to come over from the university, and we could go over there. Stuff like that. Maybe set up field trips to learn special things we wanted to know about. You probably think I'm just making all this up. But that's really why I wanted to run again. I just think school could be a lot more exciting, and I wanted to try to make it that way."

Nutty hadn't meant to get into all this. But he wasn't sure now what he had meant to say. He glanced down at his note card, and he saw the words *window peeking*, and suddenly he remembered that he did want to explain about that. And that would get him around to the *real* subject: Orlando.

"I want to say something about the window-peeking

thing—and all the other stuff that happened. See, I thought Mindy was writing all those fliers and then lying about it. So I wanted to prove it. So I was watching her house, trying to see if she went to the photocopy place or somewhere like that. But then some girls came to her house. I thought they were going to write more bad stuff about me, and I just wanted to look in and see if that's what they were doing. That's all I wanted to see. It's not like the girls were changing clothes or anything."

This got a big laugh. And Dr. Kittering whispered, "Freddie, why don't you finish up? You don't need to get into all that."

But Nutty still hadn't said what he had gone up there to say. "There's one more thing I want to say. I really don't like what happened to this whole campaign. The fliers were bad, and after a while I was ready to do anything to fight back against stuff like that. Some of us guys had a plan. We were going to plant a flier in Mindy's desk, one like the ones we thought she had been writing before. It was going to say some bad stuff about Denton, and then I was going to tear it up and act like I was some big kind of hero."

Nutty stopped for a breath. The room had gotten very quiet again.

"But I decided I couldn't do it. It was just too rotten, and too many rotten things had been going on. I just decided to go back and get the fliers and then drop out of the election. I hate all this ugly stuff that everyone's been saying about everybody else. And I don't think elections should be like that."

Nutty hesitated.

"And . . . well, anyway, sort of by accident, I found out who really had been writing the fliers. Some bad stuff had been happening, but this was the worst of all. The one who wrote the fliers was pretending to be . . ."

Nutty hesitated, and now Dr. Kittering was saying, "Freddie, please. I want you to sit down now." She had stood up behind him.

"Anyway, the one who wrote the fliers was . . ."

But Orlando's name seemed to catch in his throat. Nutty was looking at Orlando, who was ducking his head, waiting.

Nutty felt Dr. Kittering's hand on his shoulder, and he knew this was his very last chance. "The one who did it was . . ." Nutty was still watching Orlando. "The one who did it . . . did something really rotten. But I've done some pretty rotten things sometimes too. So I guess I won't say who it was. But it wasn't Mindy. And it wasn't Denton. So vote for one of them. And please don't vote for me. I just want my name taken off the ballot."

Nutty walked over and sat down. The place was silent. No one had ever ended one of these talks by saying, "Please don't vote for me."

Dr. Kittering thanked the candidates, and then she told the students to start from the back, to take their chairs and go back to their classrooms.

Mindy was sitting next to Nutty. She turned to him and said, "*See*. I told you I didn't do it."

Nutty didn't say anything.

Denton stood up and said, "Thanks, Nutty."

It was Sarah who walked over and sat down next to Nutty as soon as Mindy left the chair empty. "Wow," Sarah said. "That took some guts."

Nutty shrugged. He was just glad it was all over. He did have one image in his mind that he sort of liked. He remembered, at the last second, just before he turned to walk back to his seat, he had seen Orlando's eyes, wide and surprised, staring at Nutty.

"If you had told on the person who did it, *that* would have been mean, Nutty," Sarah said. "In front of the whole school and everything."

"He had it coming," Nutty said.

"Maybe. But you guys have been friends for a long time."

Nutty looked over at her, surprised. "How do you know who it was?" he asked.

"I knew that either he lied to you or I did. And I didn't."

"I guess I knew that too. But I still wouldn't admit it until I caught him in the act."

Nutty got up and walked off the stage. And as he did, strangely, a flash went off, and Nutty looked at a man, who had taken his picture. If Nutty had been in a good mood, he would have asked why the guy took the picture. But right now he was embarrassed and depressed. He just wanted to disappear.

chapter *11*

About ten minutes remained in the school day. The only thing left to do was go back to the classroom and vote. But Nutty couldn't get himself to do it. He figured he would probably get in trouble, but he couldn't face all the kids right now. So he slipped out the side door, and then left school by the back door. He cut across campus and went home.

But he didn't feel like hanging around the house. And the last thing he wanted to do was see Suzie when she came home. So he went to William's house. Nutty knew that William wouldn't be home yet, so he walked around to the backyard and lay down on the grass. He was afraid that if he sat in the front yard, he might have to face some of the kids from the lab school walking home.

Maybe an hour went by, and Nutty kept going over what he had done and said. He had really botched things up, in some ways, but at least he had gotten out of the whole mess, and maybe, after a while, everyone at school would forget about it.

When Nutty heard a car door slam, he got up and walked around the house. "Hey, William," he said.

"Ah, Nutty," William said, as though he were returning from deep thoughts. "So you went ahead and withdrew from the election, I suppose."

"Yeah."

"Well, it's just as well. And I guess you told everyone about your vicious mistreatment by Orlando?"

"No."

"No? Really? Why not?"

"You know why not, William. You knew I wouldn't do it."

William chuckled. "Well, let's say, I was reasonably confident you wouldn't." He reached into his pocket and found the key to his house. In fact, he had a whole ring of keys. "Should we go inside and have a glass of fruit juice—just to celebrate?"

"I don't feel much like celebrating," Nutty said.

"Why not? You had the power to destroy your friend, and you didn't. That's worth feeling good about."

"He's not my friend anymore, William."

William opened the door and the boys walked inside. "I would think he will be again," William said.

But Nutty wasn't so sure about that. He was still pretty mad at the guy.

William poured two big glasses of grape juice and the boys sat down at the kitchen table. William took a long drink and set down the glass. "So, are you out of politics forever?"

"I don't think I have any choice about that."

"Oh, well, I wouldn't say that. People have short memories. Maybe you can run for student body president at the high school. By then, you should be ready to have another go at it." He chuckled again, and crossed his arms over his chest. "And then, of course, there's president of the United States. You might want to give that a shot. I think a president named Nutty would carry a certain charm."

"No thanks. That's where they spend *all* their time saying bad stuff about each other."

"Well, yes, it does come down to something like that most of the time."

"Why, William? Why can't people just say, 'Here's what I plan to do. If you believe in those same things, vote for me.'"

"Well, they do say that. But people have gotten used to politicians promising anything to get elected. So they don't trust promises. They would rather believe accusations."

"But then the one who wins might just be the biggest liar."

"Yes, it can happen that way. I guess if the system were really pure, everyone would tell the truth, and everyone would know exactly what they were voting for, and the best person would always win. But people are people. And at least in our country, we let them be free to say what they want."

"William, it would have been a lie to plant those fliers and then pretend I was a big hero. No matter what you said the other day, I just don't think a person can lie to tell the truth."

"That's well put, Nutty. I think you've got me there. But it's also true that candidates have to know how to manage their images, use television, say the right things to the right groups—all those things. It's just the way things are."

"What if someone came along and was just really honest about everything—what would happen?"

"Well, it's hard to say. I suppose it's an image that might sell well if—"

"No, William. I mean *really* honest. What if someone ran for governor or president or something and just said, 'This is what I want to do—exactly—and I'll do everything I can to get it done'? Wouldn't people like that?"

"I sort of doubt it, Nutty. People actually demand the promises that they claim they hate."

"I don't want anything to do with it then."

"I don't blame you, Nutty. I would never want to be a politician myself."

Nutty thought about that. He took a drink of his juice and leaned back in his chair. "William, if someone paid you to help a candidate get elected, and you didn't *do* anything, but you told the candidate how to twist the truth and 'stage' phony stuff, and tear down the other candidates and everything, wouldn't you be just as bad as the one who paid you to do it?"

"Not if I were only—"

"Come on, William. If you stand in the background and tell him what lies will work, you're just as bad as the liar."

William thought for a time, and then he nodded. "Yes. I suppose so. But 'liar' is a strong word, Nutty. Some things aren't so much lies as they are—"

"If it's not true, it's a lie, William. It seems like we have to stop mixing that up."

William nodded. "Maybe so," he said. "Maybe so. Maybe it really is that simple."

Nutty finished his juice and set his glass down. There was something else he had been thinking about. "William, how did you know I wouldn't tell on Orlando today?"

"I know you. All week you've been talking about people doing rotten things—and how much you hated it. I just didn't think you could get yourself to do something that was maybe justified but awfully harsh."

"You're the one who got me thinking I shouldn't do it. You were my conscience."

"No, Nutty. You have more conscience than I do. We've already seen that. All I did was force you to think about what you were planning to do."

"Well, anyway, I guess it's good you did."

William smiled, but then he said, "Don't you need to go now?"

"Why?"

"I thought you said there was something else you wanted to do this afternoon."

"No. I didn't say that."

"Oh. Didn't you? I thought you mentioned that."

"No."

"Oh, okay. Fine." William finished the last of his drink. "Would you like some more juice?"

"No, thanks." Nutty was thinking now. "I guess you think I ought to go over and talk to Orlando?"

"Didn't you say something about that?"

"No. I didn't."

"Oh. I thought you did." William was looking quite serious, but Nutty could see the smile in his eyes.

"Hey, he still owes *me* an apology. Plus some *thanks*. I could have ruined him today."

"That's exactly right."

"I think I'll just wait to see whether he calls me. I've done my share."

"Yes, you certainly have."

"So what are you trying to say, William? Do you think I ought to go talk to him or something?"

"I didn't say that. True, he *may* be hesitating because he's embarrassed. And he *might* figure you would never forgive him. And of course, no one would *blame* you if you didn't. But it might be very difficult for him to take the first step. On the other hand, you *are* right. You've done more than your share in this whole thing."

"Okay. Okay. I'll go over there."

"Whatever you think, Nutty."

Nutty rolled his eyes. "Brother!" he said. "I'm sure glad to know you're not my conscience." And then he left.

When Nutty got to Orlando's house, he found him out in back, just sitting in his old tire swing, not swinging.

He looked surprised when he saw Nutty coming toward him. "Hi," Nutty said. "What's going on?"

"Nothing."

The next few seconds were awkward. Finally Orlando said, "I thought you weren't speaking to me."

Nutty didn't know what to say. Orlando wasn't sounding all that friendly. If Orlando didn't want to be friends, what was Nutty even doing here?

"How come you didn't tell everybody that I wrote the fliers?"

"I don't know. I was going to, but then . . . I couldn't do it."

"But you still hate me, don't you?"

"Come on, Orlando. You're the one who said all the bad stuff about *me*."

"You said it was true."

"Okay, fine. I'll see you." Nutty turned to walk away.

"Nutty," Orlando said.

Nutty stopped and looked back.

"Hey, I'm sorry."

Nutty nodded. "But why did you do it?"

Orlando was looking at the ground. He didn't speak for a time. Finally he said, "I didn't want you to be president."

"Why not?"

"If I couldn't be president, I didn't want you to be. I figured I was telling people the truth, so I wasn't doing anything all that wrong."

Nutty nodded again. "Well, that's probably right. I *was* a lousy president last year."

"Actually, this year you would have been a good one. Better than me—that's for sure."

"So you told the truth, and then I told the truth—and because of it, we lost. Denton told the truth, and he probably lost too. Mindy acted like she was a big shot, and said she cared about everything—even though everybody knows she doesn't—and she probably won. Some system, huh?"

"Well, I voted for you."

"I withdrew."

"I know. But your name was still on the ballot."

"That means I got one vote anyway."

"You probably got a few more than that."

Nutty laughed. "But don't you see what that means? I probably took a few votes away from Denton, so Mindy *did* win."

"Yeah. I'm sure that's right." Orlando looked down at the ground. "Nutty, I really am sorry. I can't believe what a jerk I was. I can't stand to think about it."

"Let's just forget about it."

"Do you really want to be friends now?"

"Yeah. I need to have someone around I can beat at basketball."

"What? You gotta be kidding." Orlando sounded serious, but then he grinned. "You know you don't have a chance against me."

"Get your ball."

"You're on."

And so Nutty and Orlando played some one-on-one for a while. Nutty beat Orlando every time, and Orlando kept saying, "Give me another chance."

But after six games, Nutty was tired. He said, "I better head home."

Nutty tossed the ball to Orlando and started to leave. But Orlando yelled to him, "Nutty, after your talk, most kids were saying you were a pretty good guy. They liked the stuff you said. So don't think everybody is going to make fun of you. It's all sort of over with now. Even the window-peeking thing."

"Well, that's good. Maybe you and I can both run for student council."

"Yeah. We could both get on, and then we could drive Mindy nuts."

"True. But I still want to get some of that stuff done that I was talking about today."

"Yeah. We'll work on that."

"Okay. It's a deal."

Nutty headed home. And he was feeling a whole lot better.

chapter *12*

When Nutty walked into his house, he saw Suzie lying on the living room floor looking at the newspaper—something he had *never* seen her do before. She looked up at Nutty with wide eyes and said, "You aren't going to believe this."

Nutty looked at the page of the paper she had open, and there was a picture of him, walking off the stage after he had given his talk, looking unhappy.

Nutty dropped onto his knees, next to Suzie. A little headline next to the picture read: Lab School Candidate Tells the Truth.

"Look what it says about you," Suzie said, and her amazement was obvious.

Nutty read the little article:

> Frederick Nutsell, better known as "Nutty" to his friends at the university laboratory school, took a unique approach to politics today. He spoke the truth.

Nutty has been running for reelection as president of the student council. But the campaign turned ugly when the mud began to fly. Negative fliers were circulated and charges and countercharges followed.

Sound like American politics?

But Nutty had had enough today. When he realized that his rival for the office, Mindy Marshall, was not the source of the negative fliers, as he had claimed, he got up before the student body, withdrew his name from the election, and then admitted his mistake. He described his own hopes that innovative teaching methods might have been developed under his leadership, but he admitted that some of his own campaign methods had been unsavory.

Nutty conceded the election to the other two candidates, but many in the school were saying, after his speech, that he might well have made a good president. In Nutty's own words, "I know I wasn't a very good president last year, but I thought I could do better if I tried again."

When was the last time you heard a politician say that? Maybe our candidates for city, state, and national offices could learn something from Frederick "Nutty" Nutsell. And maybe it's too bad he decided to withdraw his name from the election.

When Nutty had finished reading the article, he looked at Suzie. "Wow, that's weird," he said.

"I know. It was so *embarrassing* what you said today. I told some of my friends you were adopted and weren't really my brother and everything. Now I have to go back and tell them that you really are."

115

"Just tell them the real truth, Suzie."

"What?"

"Tell them I'm the finest brother in all the world." He suddenly grabbed her and gave her a big smacker on the cheek.

"Don't!" she screamed, and when she twisted away, she wiped her cheek over and over. "Nutty, don't *ever* tell anyone you did that," she whined.

"Hey, why? I'm a celebrity. I'm in the paper. I'm honest Nutty. Born in a log cabin. I'll probably run for president some day, and you'll be able to say, 'That's my brother in the White House.'"

"Yeah, right," Suzie said. "I'm the one with the talent in the family, and I *never* get my picture in the paper." She got up and strutted off to her room.

Nutty got up and hurried to the phone in the kitchen. He called William. "Have you seen the paper?" he asked.

"Yes. I read the article about you."

"Did you tell that guy to come over to the school?"

"Well, I didn't *tell* him. I merely suggested that an interesting story might be unfolding."

"But what if I had gotten up there and said all that ugly stuff about Orlando? Would he have put all that in there?"

"I don't know, Nutty. But I never worried much about that. I was pretty sure I knew what you would do."

"Well, I'm glad you did. Because I didn't."

William was amused all over again. But he kept insisting there had never really been much question in his own mind.

When Mom and Dad got home they had already heard about the article. Dad came in with five copies of the newspaper. But he was as disappointed as he was happy.

"Freddie, I'm proud of you," he said. "That honest speech you gave was perfect. But why did you withdraw? You could have won. I think playing up honesty like that was just the ticket."

"I wasn't playing it up, Dad. I was honestly being honest."

"I know. I know. And it's the right approach. But what good did it do you, if you withdrew?"

"Well, it got his picture in the paper. And everyone in town is talking about what a fine young man he is," Mom said.

"Yeah, well, that can't hurt. But if I were you, Freddie, I'd build on this. Run for president of the seventh grade next year."

"No, thanks, Dad. I'm finished with politics."

Dad started a little speech about that, but Nutty slipped away. He cut the article out of the paper, and then he read it again. He still wasn't looking forward to going to school in the morning, but the article was pretty nice. Instead of getting teased about being a window-peeker, at least he would get teased about something else.

But at school the next morning, most kids were friendly. Nutty got there just in time for school, and then hurried to his seat—to cut down on the embarrassment—but kids didn't tease him. Denton even told him he liked the article in the paper.

Nutty wished that somehow Denton could still win, but he knew there was no chance of that.

Mindy gave Nutty a sad look, as though she felt sorry for him. Nutty grinned at her, just to give her a hard time. He knew she was jealous about the article, even if she *was* about to be the new president.

Mr. Twitchell asked the students to be quiet for the morning announcements. And Dr. Kittering came on with her usual morning greeting. Everyone was expecting the announcement about the election. But she didn't mention it. And then, just a few seconds after the general announcements ended, Dr. Kittering's voice came back over the speaker.

"Mr. Twitchell, will you please send Freddie Nutsell to the office?" she said.

Twitchell nodded to Nutty, and he got up. He figured he was in trouble. Maybe she had found out that he had sneaked into the school.

Everyone watched him as he walked out, and he saw the pity in their faces. Orlando whispered, "Go ahead and tell on me."

Orlando might be right. Dr. Kittering might want to know who wrote the fliers. But Nutty was also thinking that Twitchell might have turned him in for leaving school early the day before.

So when Nutty walked into Dr. Kittering's office, he was scared. But she was smiling. That was a good sign—maybe—but it could also be her friendly way of relaxing him before she tore him up.

"Well, Freddie," she said, "that was quite a talk you gave yesterday. And an interesting article in the paper."

Maybe that was it. Maybe she wanted to know how a reporter happened to be there.

"There's something I need to find out," Dr. Kittering said.

"Okay." Now it was coming.

"Had you won the election, you had some specific goals—things you wanted to accomplish here at the school. Don't you feel bad about missing that opportunity?"

"Yeah. But maybe I'll run for student council and still work on that stuff."

"So you still want to carry out those goals?"

"Sure."

"Don't you regret withdrawing?"

"Well, it didn't matter. I couldn't have won anyway—not after all the stuff that happened."

"Perhaps. But what you asked was to have your name taken off the ballot. And it was simply too late to do that."

"Yeah, I know. I didn't think about that at the time."

"The thing is, we now have a bit of a problem."

"Why?"

"Well . . . you won."

"I *won*?"

"By a landslide."

Nutty couldn't believe it.

"I'm not quite sure what to do," Dr. Kittering said. "You asked to have your name withdrawn, but I suppose, technically, your request came too late. And since the student body voted for you—overwhelmingly—the only fair thing I can think of is to refuse your request. And that makes you the new president."

"Mindy will sue you, for sure, if you do that."

"Well, maybe. But she came in third, so I don't think she has too much to argue about."

Nutty was having a hard time accepting all this.

"So, unless you really *don't* want to be president, I'm going to announce that you're the winner."

"Maybe I should let Denton have it," Nutty said. "Maybe that would be fair."

"Well, let me ask you this. And answer me honestly." She waited for a moment. "Of the three candidates, which one do you think would get the most done this year?"

Nutty didn't have to think about that, but he didn't answer quickly—because it was embarrassing. Finally, however, he said, "I guess I would."

"I think so too. And I happen to be very happy that the kids saw who the best candidate was—in spite of all the things that happened."

Nutty was thinking maybe there was something right in the system after all. But it was strange the way it had all happened. He would have to talk the whole thing over with William and try to sort it all out.

"All right. You can go back to class. I'm going to have all the candidates come down here now, and I'm going to clarify what happened before I announce it to the whole school. I don't want an outcry from . . . well, from Mindy."

"Yeah. That's probably the best way to handle it," Nutty said, and he smiled.

Dr. Kittering smiled back, and then she shook his hand and congratulated him.

"Could you tell me one thing?" Nutty asked.

"Sure. What?"

"Who's going to be the vice-president?"

"Sarah Montag." Nutty tried not to show much reaction, but Dr. Kittering seemed to know. "I thought you might be pleased about that," she said.

Nutty got out of there.

But by the time he got halfway down the hall, he saw Sarah and the other candidates coming toward the office. He tried not to look happy. They were watching him, looking very curious.

When he reached them, he said, "Sarah, could I talk to you for a sec?"

She stopped and the others continued on, although Mindy kept looking back at them.

"Sarah," Nutty said, "something weird happened. My name was still on the ballot."

"Yeah, I know."

"Well . . . I won."

"Really?" Sarah's eyes popped wide open, and then suddenly, she was leaping toward him, throwing her arms

around him. "Congratulations!" she whispered. "That's great."

Just as suddenly, she seemed to realize what she had done. And she jumped back.

"I'm sorry," she said. "I was just . . . glad."

"It's okay."

She was turning red, and Nutty could feel his own face growing hot.

"You're going to be even happier when you hear what Dr. Kittering has to tell you."

"Really?" she said again.

"We'll be a good team," he said, and he grinned.

"Oh, wow. I gotta get down there. This is fantastic."

And off she ran.

But once she was gone, Nutty still felt something strange. A numbness. And some sense that something damp and soft had touched the side of his cheek.

Was it true? Somewhere in there, had she actually kissed him?

He really wasn't sure. But it was very nice to think that it had happened.

"Maybe politics aren't so bad," he told himself.

And then he went back to class.

But slowly he was beginning to realize. In a few minutes the whole school would know, and that would be great.

But this year, he had to *keep* his promises.